Dear Reader,

I live on a horse farm in West Texas. It's not as grand or green or plush as Quest Stables in this story, but you can believe me when I say there's always plenty of work to do. Horse people love every aspect of their four-legged critters. We're enthralled to see them born, consider ourselves privileged to raise, coddle and ride them, and feel heart-wrenching sadness when we finally have to say goodbye to them. One of our old timers here is a twenty-eight-year-old retired Thoroughbred racehorse, so when I was asked if I would like to contribute to this Thoroughbred horse-racing series, you can be sure my immediate answer was a resounding "Yes!"

I hope you're enjoying the THOROUGHBRED LEGACY series as much as I am. It seems to me it's got it all—a close-knit, multigenerational traditional family; lots of beautiful horses; plenty of romance; and a soul-searching intrigue in an international setting. A hard combination to beat, on or off the track.

I always enjoy hearing from readers. You can write to me at P.O. Box 61511, San Angelo, TX 76906. Also, please check out my Web site at www.kencasper.com.

Ken Casper

Thoroughbred Legacy

A LADY'S LUCK

Ken Casper

Silhouette® Books

Published by Silhouette Books

America's Publisher of Contemporary Romance

SILHOUETTE BOOKS

ISBN-13: 978-0-373-19925-9
ISBN-10:   0-373-19925-2

A LADY'S LUCK

Special thanks and acknowledgment are given to Ken Casper
for his contribution to the Thoroughbred Legacy series.

Visit Silhouette Special Edition and Thoroughbred Legacy
at www.eHarlequin.com.

Printed in U.S.A.

KEN CASPER

Also known as K. N. Casper, Ken Casper is an author of more than twenty books for Harlequin. He figures his writing career started back in the sixth grade when a teacher ordered him to write a "theme" explaining his misbehavior over the previous semester. To his teacher's chagrin, he enjoyed stringing just the right words together to justify his less-than-stellar performance. That's not to say he's been telling tall tales to get out of scrapes ever since, but...

Born and raised in New York City, Ken is now a transplanted Texan. He and Mary, his wife of thirty-plus years, own a horse farm in San Angelo. Along with their two dogs, six cats and eight horses—at last count—they also board and breed horses, and Mary teaches English riding. She's a therapeutic-riding instructor for people with disabilities, as well.

Life is never dull. Their two granddaughters visit several times a year and feel right at home with the Casper menagerie. Grandpa and Mimi do everything they can to make sure their visits will be lifelong fond memories. After all, isn't that what grandparents are for?

You can keep up with Ken and his books on his Web site at http://www.kencasper.com.

My special thanks to:

Toni Anderson
Beryl Liggett
Garda Parker

One

"It's no good," Brent Preston said sharply at his brother's entrance. "I've hit a wall in this investigation."

"That bad?" Andrew inquired. He poured himself a cup of coffee and sat at the marble counter in the middle of the family's country kitchen.

Brent had gone over everything in his mind and on paper a hundred times, and still he came up without answers that made sense.

He swept a hand over his face and turned to his brother. "Dammit, I don't know what the hell went wrong. That breeding went like scores of others I've arranged and supervised."

Andrew regarded him sympathetically. "No one's blaming you."

Like hell they're not. And even if they aren't, I am. I was in charge.

Last spring, three-year-old Leopold's Legacy had become the star racehorse at the family's Quest Stables, winning the Kentucky Derby, as well as the Preakness. The stallion appeared to be on his way to taking the Belmont Stakes and the Triple Crown, as well, but even without the Triple Crown, Leopold's Legacy would garner enormous stud fees. Then a computer glitch at the Jockey Association prompted a call for a certain group of Thoroughbreds to have their DNA resubmitted.

No big deal.

Until the results came back. Then all hell broke loose.

According to the new DNA test, Apollo's Ice was not the sire of Leopold's Legacy, as the registration papers stated. Even worse, no one knew who the sire was, since the DNA didn't match that of any stud in the Thoroughbred file.

The Jockey Association wasn't interested in how the mix-up had occurred; their sole concern was that the provenance of the horse was not what it was purported to be. Leopold's Legacy was pulled from the Belmont Stakes and Quest Stables was given three months to solve the discrepancy. When they were unable to do so, all Thoroughbreds majority-owned by Quest were banned by local and regional racing commissions from competing in North America. An international ban soon followed.

Almost overnight, revenue dropped by half as owners pulled their horses from the stables.

Andrew idly stirred his cup. "Listen, Brent, most of our clients will come back."

"Maybe," his brother allowed, "*if* this DNA debacle can be solved soon, and *if* it's cleared up without prejudice. But a prolonged investigation or proven fault on the part of Quest, and on me…" He let the words fade as he gazed toward the wall of windows looking out on the winter garden. Its bleakness matched his mood. "If there's no resolution at all, it'll be the end of Quest." He let out a long breath. "When I think about what Granddad has created, all his hard work, his love, his *passion*—when I think of it being wiped out in his own lifetime because I was too damn blind to know when I was being taken— I'm the head breeder. I witnessed the live cover. What are people supposed to think?"

"Look," Andrew said. "As manager of this place, I can tell you we're not going to fold. It's just a matter of time before we get a break."

He was being optimistic. Stables had gone out of business for less. He was also being generous in not mentioning how the situation was impacting his personal ambitions. Andrew had been planning to run for president of the International Thoroughbred Racing Federation someday. Brent had hoped when that happened he'd be able to take over as general manager of Quest. None of that would happen now—or maybe ever—with this scandal haunting Quest's reputation.

"I've decided to go to England," Brent announced tersely.

"England? In January?" His mother, Jenna, walked into the kitchen and hooked her favorite mug, already set out on the counter. "Dress warmly, dear."

"Why England?" his father, Thomas, asked, trailing closely behind her.

"Nolan Hunter, of course," Jenna declared, before her son could respond.

Brent almost smiled. Not much got past his mother. He had attended the Gulf Classic in Florida on New Year's Day and had run into Nolan Hunter, the owner of Apollo's Ice. Nolan had entered Sterling Pass in one of the races but was beaten in a photo finish by Brent's sister, Melanie, riding Something to Talk About. Brent had invited the Englishman to spend a few days relaxing with the family at Quest Stables in Kentucky before returning home, hoping he might learn more from him about the debacle that was threatening his family. He had, but not in the expected way.

"I'm having second thoughts about Nolan," Brent admitted.

"I thought you might be," his mother said, as she poured coffee for her husband and herself. "The man is charming and sophisticated, but there's something about him that sets my teeth on edge."

Brent nodded. "Yesterday, just before he left for the airport, I overheard him talking on his cell phone. I don't normally listen in on other people's conversations, but the tone he was using was unlike the polished English gentleman. More like a street thug."

"What was he discussing?" Andrew asked.

"I didn't get all of it. He was angry, no question about that, insisted he had things here well in hand, that there was no reason to worry. He kept referring to some third person—he didn't specify who—and said the guy couldn't do anything because he had no proof."

"Any idea who he was talking to?" his father asked.

"Someone named Camberg. The name mean anything to any of you?"

Everybody shook their heads.

"You heard only one side of this exchange," Andrew reminded him. "Isn't it possible you're misinterpreting what—"

"Of course it's possible," Brent snapped. He closed his eyes and took a deep breath. "And this conversation may not have had anything to do with Apollo's Ice or Leopold's Legacy. Nolan didn't mention horses. But I didn't mistake the guy's tone. There's a side to the Right Honorable, the Viscount Kestler, that we haven't seen before. And I'd bet good money it's not one his peers would approve of."

Andrew took a sip of his coffee. "Nolan Hunter has social position, considerable wealth and an impeccable reputation. Why would he risk all that?"

"How the hell do I know?" Brent retorted. "But he is the owner of Apollo's Ice, and until we find out who's behind the DNA fraud, he's my prime suspect."

"A trip to England might be just the thing," Jenna observed. "Especially right now."

No one needed elaboration. They were all aware that the anniversary of Marti's death was approaching.

Three years ago Brent's wife had started complaining about nonspecific problems, mostly lethargy and tiredness, nothing she could put her finger on. Athletic, bright and perpetually cheerful, she had captured Brent's heart thirty seconds after they'd bumped into each other, literally, in the college library. They'd gone together for two years before getting married right after their graduation, he with a degree in animal husbandry, she with a double major in English and sociology.

Since their twin daughters had just started kindergarten, Brent and Marti chalked her sluggishness up to her missing the girls being home all the time. He suggested she start a new project to keep herself busy.

Six months later, she died of cancer.

He'd lost her, and that loss still lay heavy on his heart, dominating his every private thought. If only he'd insisted she go to a doctor sooner… If only…

He'd spent countless hours harboring that guilt but precious few wallowing in it. He had his beautiful twins to guide through their grief and sorrow. It was a purgatory no parent ever wanted to suffer, yet it surprised him to realize that somehow he'd succeeded. He was proud of his daughters. They made him want to go on.

"What about the girls?" Jenna asked. "School starts next week."

"I'll take them with me," Brent told her. "I don't want to be separated from them right now."

"I'll talk to the school principal," his mother said. "Althea's very accommodating about children taking trips with their parents."

"Where are they this morning?" Andrew asked. "Surely not sleeping late. That'd be a first."

"They went down to the stables with Granddad to see Raleigh's Rascal, Isabella's new foal. They should be back any minute."

Just then they heard a commotion at the back door, the high-pitched excited voices of young children and the low rumble of a mature man. A moment later two identical eight-year-old girls burst into the room.

"Isabella let us touch her baby," Rhea exclaimed. "Rascal is so soft."

"And he hasn't got any teeth yet," Katie added, "just like a regular baby."

Their ponytails were held back with yellow ribbons to match the bright yellow polo shirts they were wearing with red jeans.

Their great-grandfather stood behind them. Tall and lean, with a fuzzy head of white hair, at eighty-six, Hugh Preston still had the power to dominate a room simply by walking into it.

At his heel stood Seamus, a steely-blue-gray-colored Irish wolfhound whose shoulders came to the man's knees. Hugh patted him on the head, then pointed to the corner, where the dog contentedly lay down with a slight groan to observe the activities of the humans around him.

"I figure sixteen hands," Hugh said about the foal. "A bay now, but I'm hoping he'll gray out like his sire." He poured himself coffee.

"I want orange juice," Rhea said, racing over to the marble counter and reaching for the nearly full pitcher. Katie was beside her, competing for it.

"Whoa." Brent rose from his seat. "I'll pour. First, how about showing some manners by saying good morning to your grandparents?"

"Good morning," they sang in unison.

"And Uncle Andrew," Brent prompted.

They wished him a good morning, as well. Immediately Rhea asked, "Can we have our juice now?"

Suppressing a smile, Brent poured it for them. "How would you girls like to go on a trip?"

"To Disney World?" Rhea asked, wide-eyed. "Jennifer and her mom went there over Christmas. She said it was awesome."

"I was thinking of England." He handed them each a medium-size glass only half-full.

"I don't want to go to England," Katie told him with a pout. "I want to go to Disney World."

"You'll get to see the Tower of London," Thomas told them.

"And we can hear the clock strike," Rhea contributed. "Bong, bong, bong—"

"That's Big Ben," Andrew said. "The Tower of London is a castle."

Katie frowned. "Then why do they call it a tower?"

"It's where the queen keeps all her jewelry," Jenna explained.

"You mean the queen lives in a tower?" Katie asked. "Like Rumpelstiltskin?"

"No," her sister said impatiently. "She lives in Buckingham Palace."

"But why doesn't she keep her jewelry with her at home, like other people?"

Exasperated, Rhea said, "Because she's not like other people, silly. She's the queen, and she's got so much jewelry she doesn't have room for all of it in her palace."

"When do you plan to leave?" Thomas asked his son.

"I don't want to go to England," Katie repeated, clearly not enticed by the lure of seeing a tower full of jewelry.

"In the next day or two," Brent answered, "if I can make the arrangements."

As they settled down to family breakfast, Brent mentally reviewed the other reasons he wanted to investigate Nolan Hunter, the Viscount Kestler. Over the past week Brent had learned that Marcus Vasquez, Melanie's fiancé and Quest's former trainer, was actually Nolan's illegitimate half brother. Marcus had also confided to Brent that he suspected Nolan was not being completely up front about the breeding scandal, though he could offer no proof to support his allegation. Brent might have dismissed it as sour grapes over the issue of the Spaniard's paternity, had he not overheard Nolan's phone conversation.

A horse in Dubai owned by Lord Rochester had purportedly been sired by Apollo's Ice. Not long after the Sandstone Derby, the horse was found dead. Poisoned. DNA tests revealed the stallion had not been sired by Apollo's Ice, but by the same mysterious stallion that had sired Leopold's Legacy. Brent had discussed the matter on the phone with Lord Rochester, but the Englishman had no idea who could be behind the fraud.

"What's your game plan in England?" Thomas asked, after the girls had been excused to return to the barn to see the new pony again.

"I thought I might start at the Jockey Association in London, see what I can pick up there."

"Marcus mentioned that Nolan's younger sister Devon teaches in a private girls' school near Oxford," Jenna commented. "Briar Hills Academy, I think he said. You might contact her to see what light she can shed on the situation."

"If you need help, son," Thomas said, "all you have to do is call. You know that. One of us…all of us…can be on the next available flight to Heathrow."

"I don't have to tell you to be careful, brother," Andrew said. "This scam is international and somebody's making big bucks. The closer we get to the truth, the more desperate they're going to get."

Two

The two-hour flight from Louisville to New York, followed by a three-hour layover there and another six hours crossing the Atlantic, left Brent exhausted. He'd never been one to sleep on planes, and with his twin balls of energy in tow there was no way he could have gotten a wink if he'd tried. After charming the neighboring passengers to the point of weariness, the twins settled down in front of a children's movie.

Finally he had time to review the one-sided telephone conversation he'd overheard.

"We're safe, I tell you. The bastard doesn't know a bloody thing," Hunter had said.

Was the epithet simply a crude expression, or was he

referring to Marcus Vasquez, his illegitimate half brother, who had been a trainer at Quest for a few months but left in December to become head trainer at Lucas Stables, where Brent's sister, Melanie, was currently a jockey? The two had fallen in love and were planning to marry.

"He can think whatever he bloody well wants," Hunter had protested further, "but he has no proof, so he'll keep his mouth shut, if he knows what's good for him."

Proof of what? And if he was referring to Marcus, the statement wasn't completely true. Marcus had told Brent he was convinced Hunter was behind the breeding mix-up that was destroying Quest Stables, but he also admitted he had no idea how the fraud was done, nor had he a lick of evidence to support his accusation. Marcus also confessed to hating Nolan Hunter's father for abandoning Marcus's late mother. Marcus was a damn good trainer, as Melanie's recent Gulf Classic win on Something to Talk About attested, but his emotional involvement with Hunter robbed him of objectivity, though in Brent's opinion, not necessarily credibility.

By the time the plane landed at Heathrow, they'd passed through customs and climbed into a taxi, the girls were finally showing signs of winding down. Wanting them to stay awake long enough to get to bed under their own power, Brent kept up a running narrative, pointing out the things he recognized on the trip from the airport to their hotel in London. The striking facade of the Victoria and Albert Museum. Trafalgar Square. Buckingham Palace. By the time he tucked them into bed, it was after one in the morning, local time.

He chuckled to himself. They were sound asleep before he even had a chance to pull up the covers. A three-ring circus entering the room wouldn't have awakened them now.

He poured himself a small Scotch from the bar in the sitting room and sipped it as he reviewed his plans for the next few days. Touristy stuff mostly, for the girls. He'd first come to England months ago to see Nolan Hunter right after the DNA imbroglio became known. The man had let him talk to his help, as well as take additional blood and hair samples of Apollo's Ice for further DNA testing, convincing Brent at the time that Hunter was on the up-and-up.

"Let's think outside the box, as you Americans would say," Hunter had proposed, while pouring generous quantities of fine Napoleon brandy into cut-crystal snifters, "and see if we can pull a Sherlock Holmes on this *singular* case."

To no avail. Nolan Hunter himself appeared to be uninvolved in whatever was going on. He had actually remained in England, for example, when Apollo's Ice was standing at stud in Kentucky, where Brent had witnessed the live cover that resulted in Leopold Legacy's conception.

Brent checked on his sleeping daughters. The two could be exhausting, but they were unquestionably the joy of his life. He couldn't imagine the world without them. He thought of his late wife, Marti. She'd never been to England. She would have loved it, but with two young children, they'd decided to delay any major trips until the girls were older. Now here he was alone, wishing Marti were with him.

The long day's tension gradually seeped from his tired muscles and frazzled nerves. Pouring most of the whisky down the sink, he rinsed the glass, undressed and climbed into the other queen-size bed.

He awakened to the sounds of giggling and the room flooded with light. The clock on the bedside table said nine-fifteen. The girls, to his amazement, were already dressed, Rhea sitting behind her sister on the other bed, brushing her long brown hair.

"I'm hungry," Katie said. No new phenomenon.

"Good morning to you, too," he returned with a yawn and a stretch. It had been over twelve hours since any of them had eaten. He discovered he was famished, as well.

Twenty minutes later the three of them were on their way downstairs for breakfast and a day on the town. The girls stuck up their noses at the kippered herring offered on the hotel buffet, but they decided they "really, really liked" the sausage links called bangers. He wondered if it might be because of the name.

"This bread tastes funny," Rhea said as she bit into her second triangle of buttered toast.

"Not funny," Brent corrected her. "Different. You'll find a lot of things are different here. It's one of the best parts about traveling, getting to try new and different things."

"It's good," Rhea agreed reluctantly, as she picked up another slice. "But I still say it tastes funny."

The next day they did what most first-time London tourists did. Watched the changing of the guard at Buckingham Palace. Gawked their way through the Tower of London. Craned their necks at the imposing edifices of St. Paul's Cathedral, the Houses of Parliament and Big Ben. They went to see *The Lion King,* rode double-decker buses—always on the upper level, of course—and took refuge in Victoria Station during a torrential downpour.

And then it was time to try to solve the mystery of Leopold's Legacy.

Finally, after another "proper" English breakfast at the hotel buffet, the three of them set off from Paddington Station for Oxford.

The sky was pewter and the trees bare, but once past the suburbs and outskirts of London, the English countryside took on a quaint, nostalgic quality with its Tudor houses, thatch-roofed cottages and thick-walled Norman churches. An hour later they arrived in the famous university town.

Getting a taxi wasn't nearly as difficult as comprehending what the driver was saying as he chatted with the girls along the way. What amazed Brent was that they had so little difficulty understanding his lingo, at least after the first few exchanges.

Briar Hills Academy for Girls occupied a nineteenth-century manor house of brown brick tucked neatly among low rolling wooded hills a few miles northwest of Oxford.

Brent had arranged for the visit before leaving the States, saying he was an American businessman anticipating an assignment to England in the not-too-distant future and wanted to check out schools where he could send his daughters. He'd called again yesterday from London to confirm this morning's appointment. He wasn't altogether surprised when a young lady in her early twenties emerged from the stone-arched doorway to meet them as they alighted from the cab.

"Mr. Preston?" she asked.

Stepping forward as the taxi circled around in the gravel forecourt and grumbled away, he admitted he was. "These are my daughters, Rhea and Katie."

She offered her hand. "I'm Heather Wilcot. Mrs. Sherwood-Griffin, the headmistress, asked me to welcome you and take you to her straightaway."

Beyond a small vestibule, she led them into a central hall that was dominated by a wide, gracefully curving staircase with an ornate wrought-iron banister topped with a shiny wood rail. A thick, red wool runner covered the white marble stairs, softening their ascent.

At the head of the stairs, Heather led them to a heavy, dark paneled door on the right and turned the polished brass handle. They entered a reception area.

"If you'll wait here, sir."

She went to the open doorway beyond and tapped on the framework. "Mr. Brent Preston and his daughters, Rhea and Katie, have arrived, Mrs. Sherwood-Griffin."

The woman who emerged was tall, close to six feet, and Raphaelesque in build.

"Mr. Preston," she said in a strong but pleasant voice, "how very good of you to visit us. I'm delighted to meet you." She immediately shifted her attention to the girls. "Rhea and Katie. So which twin is which?" Her smile seemed genuine.

More the extrovert, Rhea spoke up. "I'm Rhea. She's Katie."

Eyes twinkling, Mrs. Sherwood-Griffin took a minute to study the two of them, her attention flicking from one to the other. After what seemed like a very long interval, she asked, "Do the two of you always dress alike?"

"Mostly," Rhea said brightly. "Except Aunt Melanie bought us ugly green dresses. I think they look like barf, so I never wear mine. But Katie wears hers sometimes."

"I didn't bring it with me," Katie informed her. "And it doesn't look like barf. It's more like…celery pudding."

Mrs. Sherwood-Griffin's brows rose precipitously. "Celery pudding? I'll have to think about that. Rather an unusual image, I must say." She was clearly straining to control a smile. So was Brent.

"Let's go for a walk, shall we? I'll show you our grounds before it starts to rain, and you can tell me about your school back home in Kentucky."

Brent had mentioned where they were from when he'd called from the States to make the appointment. She'd obviously made note of it. The day was overcast and gloomy. The headmistress queried the girls about the subjects they were studying in school and asked questions to determine their level of advancement. Satisfied with their answers, she let them run ahead to the play area.

A scrap of paper fluttered to the ground.

"Katie, you dropped something."

One girl turned around, while the other looked over at her sister.

"Right there." Mrs. Sherwood-Griffin pointed to the ticket stub from one of the places they'd visited.

Katie stared at her, her expression one of awe bordering on fear.

"Pick it up, dear. When we go inside I'll show you where you can throw it in the dustbin."

"Yes, ma'am," Katie replied softly. She picked up the litter, then ran after her sister.

"Congratulations. We have friends at home," Brent remarked, "who've known them since they were born and still can't distinguish them."

He wondered if it was luck that she'd picked the right name or if she really could tell them apart on only a minute's acquaintance.

"Several sets of twins are in attendance here, Mr. Preston. I find them an interesting challenge."

They walked on. She recited a brief history of the school, the enrollment numbers, staff qualifications and the most recent awards the academy had received.

"When you called to make this appointment, Mr. Preston, you said you anticipated spending some time here in England on business."

"It's not certain yet. That's why I haven't said anything to the girls and asked you not to mention it in their presence. As far as they know we're here only on vacation."

"I fully understand. I've alerted the staff, as well. We have a number of foreign students boarding here whose parents travel a good deal."

He couldn't imagine leaving his girls with strangers.

"They could live with their grandparents back home, but I'd prefer to keep them with me." He paused. "Since their mother passed away, I feel it's important that we stay together as much as possible."

"My condolences on the loss of your wife, Mr. Preston. They seem well-adjusted, polite girls. May I ask why you have elected to consider Briar Hills Academy?"

"A friend recommended it. Nolan Hunter. I understand his sister is one of your teachers."

"Lord Kestler!" Her face lit up. "Yes, of course. His sister, Devon, is one of our sterling young instructors. Do you know her, as well?"

"I've never had the pleasure of meeting her."

The headmistress gazed up at the dark sky. "We'd best go inside straightaway." She clapped her hands. The girls, chattering on a seesaw, stopped instantly and swiveled to face her.

I wish they would obey me that well, Brent thought.

"Come along, girls," she called out. "Inside, quickly."

The four of them had hardly entered the building's back door when the first large raindrops began splattering the black slate walk.

"Perfect timing," Brent said, as he let the door he'd been holding close behind them.

"I'll have Miss Hunter join us," the headmistress said. "She'll be delighted to meet you. She thinks the world of her brother. A fine gentleman."

dging from the impish grin on her pixie face, the surprise would not be an unpleasant one.

Before approaching the headmistress's open doorway, however, Devon paused to adjust her frock, to make sure her belt was straight and to smooth out any wrinkles. As a matter of habit she ran her hands through her shoulder-length hair, and only then knocked on the headmistress's office doorframe and entered.

Mrs. Sherwood-Griffin was standing in the center of the room, talking to a man Devon was sure she'd never seen before. With his back to her, she saw only that he was tall, an inch or two over six feet, with impressively broad shoulders. When he turned it was his face, however, that instantly captured her attention.

He was clean-shaven with even, well-proportioned features, a slightly cleft chin and the hint of a dimple in his right cheek. His full lips had a sensual quality that seemed poised on the brink of a smile.

"Ah, Devon, there you are," Mrs. Sherwood-Griffin said in a pleasant greeting.

As she drew closer, Devon noticed the man's eyes were dark blue. They seemed the perfect complement to his tan complexion and medium-brown wavy hair. In fact, everything about him seemed perfect. She understood Heather's smile now and had to control one of her own.

"Allow me to introduce you," the headmistress went on. "This is Mr. Brent Preston, the American I mentioned in the staff meeting, who asked to visit our school."

Devon remembered now. A businessman who'd asked for an appointment because he expected to be transferred to England and was looking for a school to which he would send his young daughters.

Three

It was rare for Devon to be called out of her classroom in the midst of a lesson. She prayed it wasn't to learn of tragedy. Her mother's health was fragile, but surely Mrs. Sherwood-Griffin would come in person to inform her if something had befallen Lady Kestler. Could it be abo her brother? Nolan had become a mystery to her of la

"She has a visitor," Heather whispered, almost in a as she looked up from her desk, where she'd been tap away at her computer keyboard a moment before. said for you to go directly in."

"Who is it?" Another VIP, no doubt. Maybe a M of Parliament on an inspection tour or dropping daughter for the first time.

"You'll see."

Devon wondered at her friend's dramatic c

"Mr. Preston," the older woman continued, "may I present the Honorable Devon Hunter."

It was unusual for Sybil to introduce Devon by her title. Despite the difference in their ages and backgrounds, they were normally on a first-name basis in private. In more formal settings, such as this one, Devon became simply Miss Hunter.

She extended her hand. "Mr. Preston, I'm very pleased to meet you. Welcome to Briar Hills Academy."

His hand was large, warm and dry. She felt a slight tug as they shook. Or maybe it was her imagination. Pleased as she was to be meeting him, she had to wonder why she was here. Sybil normally handled visitors on her own without involving the teaching staff.

"Mr. Preston is acquainted with your brother," the headmistress informed her, as if reading her mind.

The mention of Nolan wasn't as welcome as it might once have been, but Devon did her best not to show it.

"I saw him over the New Year," Brent said in a deep voice that was distinctively American. She didn't fancy herself an expert on foreign accents, but she was quite certain his was what was referred to as a Southern drawl. It was fluid and mellifluous. "He had a horse running in the Gulf Classic in Florida."

Devon tilted her head to one side. "Did he win?"

Brent chuckled softly. "Actually, he lost. By a nose. To my sister."

"Your sister?"

"She's a professional jockey."

This time Devon had to laugh. "I hope he was a good sport about it."

"A perfect gentleman," Preston replied, showing even white teeth.

"And these are his daughters," Sybil said, placing her hands on the shoulders of the two girls. "Rhea and Katie."

Devon looked from one eight-year-old to the other, then folded her hands casually in front of her.

"Not fair dressing alike, girls," she said. "One of you could at least spill a bit of your breakfast porridge on your shirtwaist to make it easier."

The girls giggled.

One asked, "What's porridge?"

"Oatmeal," their father answered.

"Yuck—" her sister wrinkled her nose "—I hate oatmeal."

Devon was keenly aware of the man watching her. She liked the way his daughters looked up at him and how the one on the right—Katie?—placed her hand in his. They clearly adored the man, and he, Devon suspected, doted on them. Seeing happy families always brought bitter-sweet emotions. Her own father had been anything but sentimental. When he wasn't criticizing her, the best she could hope for was that he was mute.

"They've never been to an English primary school," Mrs. Sherwood-Griffin explained, "and are interested in seeing how it differs from theirs in America. Since Mr. Preston knows Lord Kestler, I thought perhaps you would like to show them around."

"I'd be delighted," Devon replied.

Brent was entranced. The young woman who'd entered the room was nothing short of beautiful, with dignity and charm to match. She had an oval face, cream-white flawless skin, delicately rosy cheeks and coffee-colored eyes that sparkled with intelligence and, he perceived, a hint of mischief.

When they'd been introduced and she'd placed her hand in his, he'd had an instant impulse to raise it to his lips and kiss it. He couldn't remember ever feeling that way before. It wasn't, after all, an American custom, and he wasn't even sure it was an English one, but somehow the intimacy it implied was enormously appealing.

Then he thought about Marti and felt a twinge of guilt. After exchanging a few more words with the headmistress, they left the office. Devon led them around a corner to a newer wing of the building that hadn't been visible from the front.

"How old are you, girls?" she asked the twins, who were practically skipping along beside her.

"Eight," Rhea responded.

Devon nodded, then thought a moment. "Your school system in America is different from ours. Let me see. You're in the third grade. Is that correct?"

Katie nodded enthusiastically. "Yes, ma'am."

"We start a year earlier than you, so here you would be in the fourth, but I expect what you would be learning would be about the same."

"Do you teach a particular subject, Miss Hunter?" Brent asked.

"English grammar and reading. At elementary four— your third grade—we're learning about nouns, verbs, adjectives and adverbs."

"We are, too," Rhea cried out.

"Shh." Her father put a finger to his lips. "Not so loud. We don't want to disturb the children in class."

As they walked the corridors and Devon invited him to peek into classrooms through door windows or stand at the threshold of computer-filled labs, observing young ladies flicking their fingers over keyboards and mice, Brent found himself drawn more and more to the viscount's younger sister in a way he hadn't been drawn to a woman in a long time. He asked appropriate questions, all the time trying to figure out how to bring up the one subject that had brought him there. Apollo's Ice.

She had saved her own classroom until last. When they arrived there, she took them inside and presented them to a group of twenty girls, all of whom were about the twins' age. She had just completed her introductions when a bell rang out in the hallway.

"Recess." Devon turned to the twins. "Why don't you join the girls for their break in the assembly area downstairs—it's too wet to go outside right now."

The twins didn't need a second invitation. They rushed out the door with the other girls and disappeared from sight.

"Do you get to see your brother very often?" Brent asked, using the interruption to change the subject.

"I very rarely go to London," she replied, "which is where he spends most of his time when he's not traveling. On the occasional weekend—" she placed the accent on the last syllable of the word "—when I'm able to get home to see my mother in Abbingvale, the timing always seems to be off, and he's not around."

"I thought perhaps you shared his love of horses and joined him at races," Brent observed.

For a moment she glanced at him quizzically, as though she were aware of his hidden agenda, but the expression vanished as quickly as it had appeared. "Indeed

I love horses and still ride when I'm home, but for me racing has never been the passion it's become for him."

So much for getting information from her about Apollo's Ice, Brent realized. But his interest by this point was no longer equine based. He reminded himself that his response to her was both natural and, with Marti gone, permissible, which made him wonder how he could find a way to spend more time with this young woman, the Honorable Devon Hunter.

Devon asked him questions about the girls' school until another bell sounded. The girls filed in, not as loudly as the kids back home probably would have, but with no less enthusiasm. His daughters followed, decidedly more boisterous.

They bounced up to him, faces eager. "The kids want to know if we can come back tomorrow and sit in class with them," Rhea announced to their father. "They said Miss Hunter is really, really nice."

Only young children could make friends within a matter of minutes, Brent thought. He was willing to bet it was Rhea who had led the way. Katie wasn't unfriendly or any less eager to join in groups, but she wasn't as unconditionally gregarious as her sister. Rhea was impulsive, Katie more reflective. He suspected Katie would prove the stronger personality in the long run.

"It's not up to me, girls." He wanted to give both of them a big hug for solving his dilemma. "Perhaps..." He glanced over at Devon.

"We have visitors sit in from time to time," she said, seemingly as agreeable with the idea as they were. "We must first get permission from the headmistress, of course."

"Yay! We're going to school." They clapped their hands.

"It's not certain yet, girls," their father warned.

"There are two extra seats against the back wall," Devon told them. "You may take those for now and watch, if you like, whilst your father and I confer with Mrs. Sherwood-Griffin."

While Devon spoke privately with her assistant, Brent reminded the girls to remain quiet in class and to speak only if they were spoken to by the teacher. A minute later, he and Devon left the room as the lesson recommenced.

"Funny," he said as they walked down the corridor toward the headmistress's office, "I can't recall them ever being that enthusiastic about going to school back home."

Devon laughed. "Foreign intrigue."

Speaking of foreign intrigue, he was falling under the spell of that laugh and wanted to hear more of it.

"Their mother…" she started tentatively, obviously seeking information. She was probably expecting him to say his wife had decided to stay home, maybe with other children, or that they were divorced.

"She died a few years ago."

Her shock and discomfort were palpable. "I'm so, so sorry. It must be difficult for them…for you…" Her words trailed off. A moment passed. "What about sleeping arrangements?"

Startled, he glanced over before he realized she'd intended only to change the subject. He hoped she couldn't read the thought that had instantaneously shot through his head.

"Hotel accommodations," she clarified, her pretty face tinged with pink. "You're staying in London, I presume."

"Oh…um…" He suddenly felt like a clumsy teenager. "I didn't know how late we'd be finishing up here and figured this would be a good chance to see Oxford, so I booked us into the Sword and Shield for the night."

"Good choice," she said with a nod. "Many parents visiting their children stay there. It's not especially grand, but it's convenient and I'm told quite comfortable."

"If you don't already have plans, Miss Hunter," Brent said, as they drew closer to the headmistress's office, "we'd very much like you to join us for dinner."

Four

"What do you mean, you turned him down?" Heather asked that evening. "Are you daft?"

Devon tried to ignore the question, as she gathered up the newspapers and magazines left on their sitting room settee. For the most part she enjoyed sharing a flat with her friend, but the girl could be so slovenly at times.

"For heaven's sake, why?" Heather persisted.

"He's too old for me."

"He's mature," Heather corrected her. "He's also handsome, well-mannered, and he's certainly not poor. He's also available. I heard him tell Mrs. S—"

"That his wife is dead. Yes, I know."

"Well, then?" Heather raised both her brows and grinned. "And the way he speaks makes me want to curl up on a warm bed. Really, what more could you ask?"

Devon picked up a three-day-old copy of the *Times*,

folded it and added it to the stack of things destined for the rubbish bin.

"And judging from the way those dreamy eyes of his follow you," her roommate persisted, "he's interested in more than advice on what to order from the menu selection at the Sword and Shield."

Devon continued to ignore her.

"Okay, so he's got two daughters," Heather conceded. "Twins at that. Probably not something you were bargaining for—"

"I'm not bargaining for anything...or anyone."

"But they're well enough behaved," Heather prattled on, ignoring the interruption. "They obviously love their dad, and he as obviously loves them. That counts for a lot."

Devon gave up with the paper gathering. It was busywork anyway, a diversion from listening to Heather, and wasn't doing any good. If her friend didn't say it, Devon was saying it to herself. What's more, fully half of the litter was hers.

"It's not the girls," she protested. "You know why..."

"Charles."

Devon nodded. Just the sound of his name had her muscles tightening.

"You can't allow him to dictate—"

"Stay out of it," she snapped.

"I won't." Heather seemed impervious to her friend's flare of temper. "I care too much about you to let you ruin your life this way. Besides, he hasn't called in weeks, months."

"Because I haven't been out with anyone in months."

"And who's the loser there? Keep this up and you'll be a wizened old crone who's never experienced living, much less loving. Like it or not, you're going to have to stand up to him and take control of your destiny."

"Leave me alone, will you?" Devon implored.

"I shan't."

Devon plopped down on the sofa, her arms flung out, her head thrown back against a cushion. She sighed. "I know you're right, but…"

It had started two years ago when she was still at university. Her brother, Nolan, had introduced her to his friend Charles Robinett. Charles was a duke, several steps higher up in the aristocratic pecking order than a viscount, and from a family of considerable prestige. He was young, only twenty-eight to her twenty-one at the time, a large, physically imposing ex-rugby player. Despite having broken his nose twice, he was a reasonably good-looking chap, if not exactly handsome. He was also reputed to be worth millions.

Immediately after she graduated, he proposed marriage.

For all his pedigree and fine public manners, Charles Robinett was hardly her ideal for a husband. Looks were fine, and wealth certainly made life easier. But looks faded, and she had sufficient means of her own to live a respectable life. She didn't need a man for security or social position. She certainly didn't need one who was a tyrant, who demanded unquestioned compliance with his wishes without any consideration of her desires or interests.

When she rejected his offer, he swore he'd do physical violence to any man she showed an interest in. She took it as bluster at the time, the idle petulance of someone who was used to getting his own way without much effort on his part. After all, he was a duke. Then her next two dates were mugged after delivering her home. The first time she could dismiss it as coincidence, but the second established a pattern. The assailants were never apprehended, so there was no way to link the attacks to Charles, but Devon knew he was behind them, especially after he called her to renew his threat. She got the message.

"You know what happens when you give in to a bully," Heather stated now. "He becomes more demanding."

Would Brent Preston welcome a chance to play Sir Galahad? Devon wondered.

That was what she'd expected of her brother when she reported Charles's threat to him. She was sure he'd warn the duke off. Instead Nolan had called her foolish for passing up such a rare opportunity to climb the social ladder. He'd dismissed Charles's "supposed" threats as a misunderstanding on her part, declaring instead that in his opinion she should take what the man said as a compliment and proof of his devotion to her.

Devon had been at once stunned and furious that her own brother, whom she'd idolized for so many years, would in effect call her a liar and fail to even investigate a situation which potentially put her in harm's way.

Since then their private relationship had been distant and strained, if not quite crossing the threshold to hostility. In public and in the presence of their mother they played their accustomed roles, even joking the way they had in the past. Devon didn't know what had come over her brother, but the change in him saddened her greatly.

"I know you're right," she told Heather. "But I'm not sure it's fair to put Mr. Preston in that sort of position."

"You're going to have to stand up to Charles sooner or later, you know. Why not with a man who looks like he can take on half of rugby union single-handedly?

Besides," Heather added, "he's not going to be here very long. This is just an exploratory trip in case he gets that job transfer."

Devon finally laughed. "Perhaps I ought to sell tickets."

Heather slouched onto the sofa beside her and grinned. "I'll buy one."

Brent and the girls ate dinner—roast beef and Yorkshire pudding was their current favorite—at the hotel that evening after walking around Oxford and seeing a few of the more famous landmarks of the university town. He soon realized, however, that eight-year-old girls weren't interested in or impressed by ancient seats of scholarship.

To his own chagrin he found himself a bit bored by it all, as well, without adult companionship. He kept thinking of Devon Hunter. She undoubtedly knew all about the things he was seeing and could show him more. In his mind he pictured her eyes lighting up, her lips smiling, as she recited a concise history of the courts of learning, including ancient tales of duels and chivalry.

It was foolish really. He'd met Devon only briefly, and she'd turned down his dinner invitation. He also had to remind himself he wasn't here for the sightseeing or to pursue the opposite sex. The world might see him as unattached, but he still thought of himself as a married man. At least he had until meeting Devon Hunter.

To his relief, after dinner he found a movie on television that the twins were actually able to agree on. The true sign of their tiredness, however, was that they didn't put up much of a fuss when he told them it was time to go to bed. They'd been on the go for several iend. "So many people in Oxford know me. Word is ound to get back to him that I was in the company of a good-looking American gentleman…."

"And his two kids," Heather pointed out.

"That won't make any difference."

Charles was jealous and vindictive, and his threatening telephone calls since their breakup had made it clear he didn't want her seeing other men and would take vengeance on any man who shared her company.

"He has no bloody right laying claim to you like that," Heather countered angrily. "He asked you to marry him and you said no. That should be the end of it. You can't spend the rest of your life cowering in fear of a man whose designs on you border on the criminal and perhaps even the psychotic."

"You're not telling me anything I haven't already told myself," Devon murmured as she slipped out of the dress she'd worn at school and went to the lavatory. For the past two years she'd been alone and lonely. She could change that if she'd cease being such a coward and a victim. She used to be popular, outgoing.

Her determination to disregard Charles's threats was intractable until she thought about Brent's children. Surely Charles wasn't so depraved, so obsessed with her, that he'd do them harm. The girls had already lost their mother. If something were to happen to their father, something that resulted from her association with him, she'd ever be able to live with herself.

Wearing only bra and panties, she weighed the pros cons of the situation as she scrubbed her face. She erged a minute later in her dressing gown, sat at her ty and brushed out her shoulder-length hair. While

days and the pace was finally taking its toll. Within five minutes of their heads hitting the pillows, they were sound asleep.

He, too, was weary, but he was even more restless. He got out his laptop and continued his search of the Internet for information about the Hunter family. Nolan, he discovered, was the sixth Viscount Kestler. His father, Nigel, had left him the title eight years earlier, when he died at the age of fifty-two of kidney failure, according to one report. Another version alluded to the condition being the result of chronic alcoholism. His wife, Sarah Morningfield Hunter, the mother of Nolan and Devon, apparently came from the landed gentry rather than the aristocracy. The current Kestler estate, Morningfield Manor, was from the distaff side of the family. Brent couldn't find much about Sarah Hunter, except one article which noted that she was two years older than her late husband and that she was in frail health because of a heart condition.

By the time Brent turned off the computer and prepared for bed, he didn't know much more than he had before, nothing, at any rate, that shed light on his investigation into the mystery of Leopold's Legacy's DNA.

The entire evening would have been far more pleasurable, and perhaps more productive, he decided, as he slipped in between the sheets, if Devon had agreed to spend it with them.

He shouldn't be thinking about a beautiful young woman while he was lying in bed, and in particular he shouldn't be thinking about Devon Hunter. His research had disclosed her age, twenty-three, a dozen years his junior. Quite a gap. Yet, when he was in her company, she seemed his match in maturity. He didn't feel more than a decade older. If anything, she had the opposite effect. She made him feel ten years younger.

From her remarks, it appeared unlikely she had anything to do with her brother's fraudulent activities, or that she was even aware of them, assuming her statement that she rarely had contact with him was true. Her expression seemed to have clouded over when she'd spoken about him. Protectiveness or duplicity? Why would Nolan need protection? As for duplicity, could she be aware that her brother was engaged in some sort of fraudulent dealings and simply didn't know the details or didn't want to?

In any event, she wouldn't be pleased when she discovered Brent suspected him of criminal behavior. Under the circumstances, entertaining notions of a closer relationship with her was a foolish distraction and a waste of time. Unfortunately, some reactions weren't subject to reason.

The next morning the girls were wide-awake before he was and doubly full of life. A good night's sleep had invigorated them. To his relief and amazement, their enthusiasm for going to school hadn't diminished overnight, which meant he would have an opportunity to see Devon again when he dropped them off and once more when he picked them up.

They ate another hearty English breakfast and set off for the academy.

By arrangement the previous afternoon, he delivered them directly to Devon's classroom. Along the way the girls kept babbling on about how nice Miss Hunter was, how all the girls in the class liked her, that she wasn't mean like some of the teachers back home—a charge he couldn't remember hearing before—and how much they were looking forward to spending the day in her class-

room. Apparently, Brent reflected, Devon was [...] spell on his children, as well.

She greeted him with a smile and told the girl[...] to sit. Wisely she didn't keep them together but [...] them off with different partners.

"You may collect them at three o'clock. If they'[...] downstairs, they'll be up here with me. How are [...] planning to occupy your time alone?" she asked casu[...] then, as pink rose to her cheeks, excused herself. "[...] was impertinent of me. I beg your pardon."

His response was mixed. He found her discomfo[...] amusing, even encouraging. On the other hand, complet[...] honesty on his part would be unwise.

"I have business research I need to do, so this time off works out nicely. What time do you quit today?"

She gazed at him in a way that made him wonder if it was with interest or dismay. He preferred to think it might be the former. "It's Friday," he reminded her. "I thought we might stay here another night, if you'll agree to join us. Our attempt at playing tourist yesterday wasn't ver[...] successful. We ended up watching television."

"Oh, my." Her brown eyes sparkled with exagger[...] dismay. "That bad?"

"And the offer of dinner is still open."

She grew more serious, but the humor didn'[...] pletely fade, and that gave him hope.

"Please join us," he repeated.

Whilst changing clothes in her flat late th[...] Devon debated with herself and Heath[...] wisdom of spending the evening with Bre[...]

"Charles has spies everywhere," sh[...]

she was applying a dusting of makeup, Heather inventoried the small collection of perfumes on the dressing table and selected one.

Devon couldn't help smiling as she dabbed it behind her ears. It had been so long since she'd been out with a man, the prospect sent little shivers tripping along her skin and in her belly.

"What are you wearing?" Heather asked. "Something simple, I should think. Casual but elegant, of course."

Devon laughed. "I was considering the dark green trousers and the silver-gray blouse."

"And your rust-colored cable-knit pullover. Perfect. Oh, wait."

Heather rummaged in the side drawer of Devon's dressing table and brought out a necklace of polished black-, green- and wine-colored stones and a matching bracelet.

"Here. Where's your good watch?"

If Devon weren't already keyed up about her date, her friend's enthusiasm would have made her excited. She pointed to the little drawer under the mirror. Heather extracted the stylish gold timepiece with its tiny diamond chips for numbers.

Ten minutes later Devon spun around in front of the mirror that ran the length of her wardrobe. She was feeling giddy, like a girl let loose after a long confinement.

Pleased with the results thus far, she now considered her footwear.

"The black boots," Heather insisted.

Devon agreed. Finally she put on her tan Burberry and grabbed a multihued green silk scarf.

"Wish me luck," she said as she went to the door.

"I wish you more than that. I'll want a full accounting when you get back—" Heather smiled "—whenever that may be."

Devon left the flat laughing.

Five

The ornately carved grandfather clock in the corner of the lobby was striking six when Devon walked into the old Tudor inn. At this time of year the sun had long set.

Brent and the girls were waiting for her on the settee in front of the fireplace, in which a lively fire burned. Unlike so many Americans who dressed casually for nearly every occasion, he was wearing a perfectly tailored chestnut tweed jacket, a fawn shirt and olive-green tie. His darker sepia slacks were sharply creased and he had on comfortably worn polished brown loafers.

He was even handsomer in this more informal attire, she decided, than in the proper suit he'd had on earlier in the day. But it was the man and not the clothes that caught her attention—and her imagination.

He was powerfully built. She wondered what sports he played, convinced that whatever they were, he played them well. Brent Preston didn't strike her as a man who did things by half measures.

"My," she said, making an effort to focus her attention on the twins instead of him, "aren't you the smart duo?" They were dressed in matching pink frocks and mid-calf boots.

The girls jumped up and ran to her, clearly pleased to see her. As delighted as she was with their greeting, it was their father's appraisal that warmed her insides.

"Where do you suggest we eat?" Brent asked.

"There are several places in the area," she said. "The Stag and Steer, a short walk from here, is quite good. Their roast beef and Yorkshire pudding are excellent—"

"Yay, roast beef and Yorkshire pudding," Rhea sang out.

"I want something else," Katie complained. "I'm tired of roast beef and Yorkshire pudding."

"Well—" Devon put a finger to her chin "—they have steak pie, mutton chops, their trout is quite good and—"

"Steak pie," Katie repeated. "I want steak pie."

Brent smiled. "I guess it's the Stag and Steer then. Trout, you say…"

They donned their coats.

"Thank you for joining us," Brent said as they walked through narrow streets to the restaurant. "It's always more fun to have someone local show us around."

Devon smiled. "And it's my pleasure to be that someone."

It *was* a fun meal. Brent, Devon soon discovered, was possessed of a droll sense of humor. He told stories about life in Kentucky that made her wish she were there.

"Is the grass really blue?"

He chuckled. "It's definitely lush and definitely green, but it's not even native to America. It grows all over Europe and North Africa."

She sighed dramatically. "Another myth destroyed."

Taking a different route back to the hotel after dinner, they came upon a toy shop that featured old-fashioned porcelain dolls. The girls were fascinated by their painted faces and period costumes. They begged their father to bring them back the following day.

"Tomorrow's Saturday," he pointed out. "They probably won't be open."

Devon could tell he was teasing, but the twins apparently didn't realize it. Rhea screwed up her mouth with annoyance and Katie stared stoically, her eyes teary.

"I believe they're open until noon," Devon informed them.

"Please, can we come back?" Rhea begged. "Please?"

He turned to Devon. "If you'll join us."

She hadn't anticipated that. Or had she subconsciously been angling all along for another excuse to see him?

"If you really want me to."

"We really want you to," Brent said quietly. His lips said "we," but his eyes said "I." Awareness set off little flutters in her belly.

At the hotel, he invited her up to their suite. Since the inn was nearly empty he'd been able to book their best and biggest accommodations.

She hesitated.

"Will you help tuck us into bed?" Rhea asked eagerly.

It was an unusual request, one she'd not received before, and the intimacy it implied made her slightly uncomfortable. She glanced at Brent. All evening long they had been catching each other's eye, then looking away. Heather had been right, Devon realized. He was interested.

Were it not for her concern about Charles, she would have accepted the invitation with alacrity. She enjoyed this man's—and his daughters'—company and would very much like to share more of it.

But Charles—

If she was surrounded by spies for the duke, as she suspected, he would know she'd been in Brent's company. Not going up to his room wouldn't make any difference, regardless of his young daughters being with them. Charles had made it clear he didn't want any other man to enjoy her companionship in public or in private.

Then she took another look at Brent and couldn't imagine him being intimidated by anyone, even a man like Charles. Besides, in a few days Brent Preston would be on his way back to the United States. Charles wasn't likely to pick a fight with him across the Atlantic.

"Just for a few minutes," she said to the girls, then added to Brent, "if that's all right with you."

All right? Brent felt his blood racing, long-dormant sensations tingling. Thoughts and desires he'd managed to bury since Marti died were resurfacing with brutal vengeance.

He and Devon had spent the evening like two old friends, exchanging ideas, asking each other questions, sharing laughter. Twice he'd spontaneously reached for her hand, found it and squeezed. Twice she'd willingly returned the casual caresses. More than like *friends*.

Guilt rampaged through him. If Marti were here, he would never…

But she wasn't, and the renewed realization that she

was gone forever produced an ache so acute it could have brought him to tears. Then he raised his head—till then unaware he'd been staring at the ground—and saw Devon, and a different kind of ache possessed him. For a fate-changing instant he prayed that Marti would understand, and if he was making a mistake, forgive him.

There was such warmth in Devon's smile that he had to believe that Marti would approve.

They took the stairs up one flight to what the British and Europeans insisted on calling the first floor, as if the ground floor didn't count. The suite comprised two modest bedrooms, a private bath and a sitting room with a small marble fireplace.

"Change into your jammies," Brent told the girls, "and brush your teeth, then I'll come and tuck you in."

"We want Devon to tuck us in, too," Rhea reminded him.

"She will. Now, go get ready for bed."

The twins danced into their bedroom. After a few seconds he and Devon could hear water running in the bathroom.

"I like them, Brent. Very much. They're wonderful children."

"I guess I'll keep them then," he replied, more aware of her and the effect she was having on him than the lighthearted words tumbling out. "You've made quite a hit with them, too."

"We're ready," Rhea called out a minute later.

"Come on," Brent said, and put his hand on the small of Devon's back as he guided her toward the girls' bedroom.

Brent hugged the twins, gave them each a kiss. Devon could remember her father sending her to bed, but she couldn't recall him ever kissing her good-night, much less tucking her in. How lucky these girls were to have a father who loved them. She expected to simply say good-night and leave, but they insisted on giving her a hug and kiss, as well.

"Pleasant dreams," she said in a voice choked to a whisper as she watched them snuggle contentedly under the covers.

What a wonderful experience it was to hold the children in her arms and kiss them good-night. She had no siblings other than Nolan, who was so much older that he hardly counted. She had a few cousins, but they, too, were his age, so she had been brought up virtually as an only child and never experienced the kind of intimacies this family, incomplete as it was, engaged in as a matter of routine. She envied them.

Family dynamics in her life had been keeping track of how much her father was drinking, and if necessary, avoiding him. Her mother, who had been over forty when Devon was born—an unplanned, if not unwanted child— had been frail for as long as Devon could remember, owing to a wonky ticker, as her father had invariably phrased it. At one stage Devon had wondered if Sarah Hunter wasn't faking feebleness to gain attention, but entertaining such a doubt had only made her feel guilty.

The warmth of this encounter with the Prestons, father and daughters, filled her with a longing she'd never felt before. If this was what it was like to have a *normal* family, she decided, she wanted it. She'd thought of family before, many times, but somehow the image had never included moments like this.

Brent stood behind her in the doorway to say their final good-night, his body's warmth enveloping her, as his arm reached around her and pulled the door closed.

Six

He was on his feet so quickly she almost fell into the void he left. She regained her balance and stood up as he darted to his daughters' bedroom and shot inside. Devon went as far as the door but didn't enter.

Rhea was sleeping soundly, her face turned away from the light coming in through the open doorway. It was Katie who was crying.

Brent sat at her side and ran his hand gently along her hair and down her neck.

"What's the matter, pumpkin? Having a bad dream?"

"I miss Mommy."

He gathered her in his arms. "I know, honey. I do, too. But you know she's here with you. You just can't see her."

Katie cried harder against his chest. "Daddy…"

"They'll be sound asleep in no time," he assured her with a smile, and the love she saw in his eyes made her all but cry out with the pain of her own loneliness. "They run at top speed all day, then it's like turning off a light switch, and they sleep the sleep of the dead."

She didn't like the metaphor, but she smiled nonetheless and shivered a little.

"You're cold." As if it were the most natural thing in the world, he wrapped an arm across her shoulders.

The tremor that flowed through her now had nothing to do with the room's chill but everything to do with the heat his touch generated. His body was solid, his contact firm and reassuring, and she wanted to burrow into it.

She tried to tell herself she was reacting like an adolescent. In truth, his embrace reinforced her awareness of the two years she'd spent alone, untouched, a woman apart.

"Let me light the fire," he said, "then I'll pour us a glass of something."

She wanted to cry out "no," when he released her. Instead she stood where she was and watched him bend down and reach for the propane starter to ignite the gas log.

He stood up, smiling at her, then walked over to the drinks table in the corner. "Let's see. Scotch, of course. Brandy. Cream sherry. There's red wine. What can I get you?"

Another hug, please, she wanted to say. "Sherry, I think."

"Sherry, it is. I'll have Scotch. I'm a Bourbon man at home."

"Kentucky is famous for its Bourbon whisky, isn't it?"

"We make the best. I've heard Tennessee produces some passable stuff, too, but I'm partial to the home spirits."

"Naturally."

He caught the humor in her voice, looked over and grinned.

"I have to thank you for a wonderful day," he said, pouring a couple of ounces of sherry into a wineglass.

"Your girls are enchanting." What she really felt like saying was that she didn't want the day to end. "You must be very proud of them."

"I am." He decanted even less whisky into a short tumbler for himself. "You have to understand, though, they've been on their best behavior the last couple of days, for which I'm enormously grateful. But they can also be holy terrors, I assure you."

She smiled as he handed her the sweet wine.

"Thanks for inspiring them," he said.

"It's I who should be thanking you for today," she replied, standing in front of the fire. "You've given me a special gift, sharing your family and allowing me to see the world 'round me with fresh eyes. I shan't forget that."

He loved listening to her speak, the crisp accent that was so clear and precise, the unaccustomed words. Meeting her eyes, he held up his glass. "To special gifts."

She raised hers, never breaking eye contact. The intimacy of the moment lingered even after they'd sipped their drinks.

Taking her hand, he led her over to the love seat in front of the fireplace. Yellow and blue flames licked around the simulated logs. The fire wasn't giving off much heat yet, but that wasn't important. There was already enough between them.

"You must be tired," she said softly. "This has been a long day for you, too."

"All I feel right now is contentment. It's been a wonderful two days," he murmured. "I met you."

She looked up at him then, her eyes searching brought his lips down to hers, and suddenly the hea fireplace was nothing compared to the heat betwee

It was all happening so fast, she thought, y quickly enough. She closed her eyes, let her senses A furor of needs and desires raged inside her. Was i man who was setting her free? Or would any man tou ing her have provoked the same response?

She sensed, too, the desperation in the kiss. Were th no more than two lonely people starved for contact?

They broke off. He didn't look at her but bowed hi head. Had she disappointed him? Did he feel regret?

Another long moment elapsed before she was aware of a sound coming from the other room, a muffled sob.

B

"What is it, baby?"

"Are you going to take us back to that school and leave us there?"

"What?" He held her gently away so he could look into her tear-drenched eyes. "What are you talking about, honey?"

"The other kids…they told us their parents brought them there and left them. They don't see them anymore, except on visitors' day. They don't go home anymore, except maybe on holidays. Are you going to leave us there, too?"

He thought he'd known pain before, but nothing compared with the agony he felt at that moment. For his girls to think he would abandon them…

He hugged her so tightly he was afraid he was going to hurt her.

"I would never do that, sweetheart. I love you so much, I could never leave you with other people. We're only visiting here. When our vacation is over we're going home again. All of us. Together."

She sobbed. "I was afraid you didn't want us with you anymore."

"Shh," he soothed. "That's not true, honey. It'll never be true."

He rocked her in his arms and felt his own tears roll down his face.

"We're going to have a good time while we're here," he said, "then we're going home. Okay?"

She nodded and hiccupped and clung to him all the tighter.

"I promise." He brushed away her tears with the pad of his thumb and kissed her cheek softly.

He urged her to lie down again, pulled up her covers and sat on the edge of the bed until she had fallen asleep. Only then did he tiptoe from the room.

Devon watched him pick up his whisky glass with a shaky hand and swallow its meager contents. She waited for him to go to the drinks table and refill it. Wasn't that what men did when things went wrong or they didn't get their way? Take another drink? To her amazement and relief, he didn't.

"What's going on, Brent?" she asked in a quiet but determined tone.

He spun around, as if he had forgotten she was there. "I should have realized something was bothering her," he said morosely. "Rhea is the chatterbox, but Katie isn't usually as withdrawn as she was this evening."

"That doesn't answer my question."

He finally looked at her. "What do you mean?"

"You obviously didn't come to Briar Hills Academy with the intent of enrolling your daughters there, unless what you told Katie was a lie."

"It wasn't." He opened a bottle of Evian water and poured the contents into a clean tumbler.

"So why did you come to the school?" When he didn't respond, she ventured further. "Are you going to tell me, Brent? Or should I just leave?"

"Don't go. Please."

He sounded so earnest, so troubled, but he had already lied to her once. Why should she believe anything he told her now? Had the kiss been a lie, too? A way of manipulating her, of getting whatever it was he was after? She could still imagine the sensation of his lips on hers.

e laughed without humor. "I had the test repeated, but
results were the same. I talked to everyone who had
he in contact with the stallion and the mare. I even flew
r here and talked with your brother. He helped all he
uld, even let me draw new blood and hair samples from
pollo's Ice for testing, but it did no good. Apollo's Ice
as not the sire we paid for. Your brother claimed to have
io idea what could have happened. He pointed out that
he hadn't even been in the States at the time of the
breeding, whereas I had had complete and uninterrupted
custody of the mare."

"I don't understand," Devon said. "It sounds like Nolan
cooperated with you in every way possible, so why are
you here? Why are you accusing him of wrongdoing?"

Brent refreshed his drink, taking only half of what he
had earlier, then gazed at its amber glow in the glass and
put it down. He retrieved his Evian and drank that instead.

"In spite of what he said, I think your brother was
involved in this fraud. I spent today reviewing records,
files, newspaper articles—you have excellent research
facilities here at Oxford. I was trying to learn everything
I could about your brother's equestrian interests. There
have been other frauds involving Apollo's Ice. I'll say
this, too. Nolan has covered his tracks very well."

She stared at him for a long minute, her lips pursed,
then she rose from her chair.

"I'll tell you what it sounds like to me, Mr. Preston. I
hink you have made a cock-up of your breeding business
nd now you're looking for a scapegoat."

"Please sit down," he said, "and I'll tell you."

She wasn't sure she should stay, but she did want
answers, and he was the only one who could furnish
them. She settled into the club chair. Her sherry was
within reach, but she ignored it.

"What do you know about Apollo's Ice?" he asked.

She cocked her head and studied him. After a long
pause she replied, "Apollo's Ice. Is that a horse?"

He nodded and sat on the sofa where they'd been
kissing a few minutes earlier. "Yes, a stallion your brother
had up for stud in the States four years ago."

"I told you I don't know anything about his horses. Or
do you think I lie as facilely as you do?"

"I'm sorry I deceived you, Devon. Maybe after I've explained what's happened—"

She swallowed a sarcastic reply and folded her arms
across her chest.

"My grandfather, Hugh Preston, came to the United
States from Ireland more than sixty years ago," Brent
said. "He worked hard, saved his money, invested in a few
promising ponies, did well and eventually married my
grandmother. Together they bought a thousand acres of
prime Kentucky farmland and started Quest Stables."

He took a sip of his water and put the glass back down
next to her sweet sherry on an end table.

"It's done well over the years. We're not the biggest
horse farm in Kentucky anymore, much less the country,
but we're not exactly small, either. We have... We had an
average daily horse population of five hundred and a per-
manent staff of nearly seventy-five employees.

"Granddad retired from active management of the
business after my grandmother passed away a few years

back, leaving day-to-day operations to my father, who more recently has turned over details of the business to my brother and me. Andrew is the general manager. I'm in charge of breeding."

She listened without interrupting or showing emotion. Rising, he went to the drinks table and splashed more Scotch into the whisky glass he'd abandoned. Remaining by the window, he leaned against the sill, facing her.

"Four years ago, when I learned Apollo's Ice was going to be standing stud at Angelina Stud Farm about fifty miles from us, I booked one of our premium mares, Courtin' Cristy, to be bred to him. The results were outstanding. Last year the foal, Leopold's Legacy, won the Kentucky Derby as well as the Preakness and appeared to be on his way to taking the Belmont Stakes and the Triple Crown."

He swallowed some of his drink and made a face. "It's going to take me a while to get used to the taste of this stuff." He put it aside.

Devon waited, knowing the comment was a delaying tactic. She was having a hard time reading his face. Anger, yes, but there was something more complex there, as if he couldn't figure out who or what he was angry at.

"Then came a computer glitch at the Jockey Association. A small group of DNA files were lost or corrupted, so the association requested that the owners of the affected horses draw new blood samples." He took a deep breath. "A simple enough procedure. No problem, right?"

He gulped the remainder of his whisky. "Except according to the results, Apollo's Ice was not the sire of Leopold's Legacy. Overnight we were branded as frauds."

Now his anger spilled over.

"Do you have any idea what impac[...] had?" he demanded.

She shook her head, unwilling to speak[...]

"No," he snapped, "I don't suppose y[...] me tell you."

He began to pace, his head lowered, his [...] fierce. "A major source of our income is from[...] and training fees. Breeding brings in big money[...] it's only for three months a year. Because all Th[...] breds officially have their birthdays on January fi[...] one wants a foal born late in the year. When the que[...] of Leopold's Legacy's provenance came up, he [...] banned from further competition until the discrepan[...] is corrected, and three months later, when we have n[...] resolution, all Thoroughbreds majority-owned by Ques[...] Stables were banned from competing in North America. An international ban followed in October."

That didn't seem unreasonable, she wanted to argu[...] given they had proof. The DNA. But she said nothing[...]

"As a result," he continued, "owners immediately beg[...] removing their racehorses from Quest. Horses that w[...] there for training were taken away, as well. Bree[...] contracts dried up overnight, and suddenly we were f[...] with big cash-flow problems."

"I'm sorry."

"Employees who depended on us for their livelih[...] grooms, trainers, exercisers, stall muckers, groun[...] ers, farmers, maintenance crews—had to be let [...] because I bred a mare to a stallion your brother[...] to be Apollo's Ice but wasn't."

"Surely there was something you could do to [...] accusation wrong."

Seven

"No, Devon, I'm not looking for a scapegoat." Brent ran a hand through his hair, ready to vent his anger, but she was so young and pretty, and the innocence he saw in her soft brown eyes made him feel instant regret for any doubts he'd harbored that she might be involved with her brother. "I'm looking for the culprit." He finished the sentence more gently than he'd started. "And I have good reason to think it's your brother."

"But no evidence," she reminded him. "Otherwise you would have gone to the authorities?"

"I don't have any proof," he was forced to acknowledge, "but I do have serious suspicions."

"Suspicions are cheap," she scoffed. "I think you're looking for someone to blame for your own incompetence."

He absorbed the insult without fighting back. Hadn't he accused himself of the same thing? She was defending her brother, her family's proud name, something he could understand and respect. The question was whether she was doing it blindly or if she had good reason to think Nolan innocent of wrongdoing.

"I'm not alone," he said. "Your half brother is convinced Nolan's involved in the fraud, too."

Her angry glare transformed instantly to one of shock, then confusion. "Half brother? What are you talking about? I don't have a half brother. There's just Nolan and me."

Brent shook his head, not surprised by her reaction. Nolan had made it abundantly clear to Marcus Vasquez that he had no intention of acknowledging his bastard sibling. The question now was whether Devon was mimicking her brother's attitude or if she really didn't know about her father's other child. Brent suspected ignorance, which would further confirm her lack of involvement in Nolan's activities.

"I'm sorry to be the one to break this to you, Devon, but that's not true. You do have a half brother—his name is Marcus Vasquez. He's currently the trainer at Lucas Stables in Kentucky, but he was our trainer at Quest for a while. He and Nolan were both at the race in Florida on New Year's Day. They weren't exactly pleased to see each other."

She jumped out of her seat and glared at him, her delicate hands bunched into tight fists. "I don't believe you."

He decided not to upset her further with an account of how Marcus had saved his sister Melanie's life after the race and ended up killing the attacker in self-defense. Brent couldn't prove there was a direct link between the attack and the breeding fraud he was investigating, but the connection seemed inescapable. It also established the people involved felt threatened enough to resort to attempted murder.

As for Devon, learning she had an illegitimate half brother was shock enough. He softened his gaze and lowered his voice sympathetically. "I know you don't, or at least you don't want to believe me, but it's true."

He moved closer and unfurled the fingers of her right hand, bringing it up to his lips to kiss.

"Ask Nolan." He led her back to the chair and sat at an angle to her on the sofa, still clasping her trembling fingers. "He'll tell you it's true. Before Nolan was born your father had an affair with Marcus's mother. He didn't tell her he was married until she announced she was pregnant, and then he deserted her. They had no further contact. On her deathbed, she sent Marcus to him with a plea that he come to see her one last time before she died. Apparently she was still in love with him. Your father refused, claimed he didn't even remember the woman. Marcus then approached Nolan and appealed to him to intercede with your father, but all Nolan did was tell Marcus to get lost and never bring up their supposed relationship again."

As Brent was speaking to her, Devon bit her lips. Her eyes grew watery with sadness. The picture he was painting was disturbingly cruel and heartless on the part of both her father and brother.

"I can believe it of my father," she muttered. "He was a cold, selfish man. But I can't believe my brother knew about this and never told me."

"I'm sorry you're finding out this way. I really am. I have no idea if your mother knows—"

Devon shook her head dejectedly. "I don't know what

it was about my father. I never found a good reason to love him, except out of duty, but my mother did, even though he treated her abysmally. I doubt this poor creature you just mentioned was my father's only liaison, but if my mother had learned he had other children… If she were to find out even now, I think it would kill her."

Devon slouched in the seat, threw her head back against the chair cushion and stared, glassy-eyed, at the ceiling. Still holding her hand, Brent swung around and knelt at her feet, gently taking her other hand in his. She'd just had a terrible shock and must deal with it privately before she would be ready to accept consolation from another person, but that didn't mean she had to be alone, a conclusion she acknowledged by squeezing his fingers with desperate strength.

Suddenly, as if rebelling against the emotional blows she'd received, she jumped up, nearly knocking him over.

"What the hell has any of this got to do with your damn horse?" she exploded bitterly.

"Directly, nothing," he admitted calmly and rose to his feet. "But I've come to realize that there's more to your brother than the social sophistication he shows the world."

Brent nearly smiled at the fire he saw in those beautiful brown eyes now. Fire and fight. A lusty combination. Heaving in a big breath, she sat down again in her chair.

"You have no proof Nolan was involved in this breeding…mistake—"

"Fraud."

She flinched at his uncompromising tone.

"You've been peddling a pack of lies since you arrived here," she said in a seething tone to keep her voice down. "You didn't come here in anticipation of a business transfer. You weren't looking for a school for your girls. For all I know you may not even be a widower."

"I am," he said, all too aware of the tears in her eyes and how much he had hurt her. "I may be capable of deceiving with words, but that kiss wasn't a lie, Devon, not what I feel for you."

"I wish I could believe you."

"You can, and you will if you listen to your heart. I wasn't making anything up when I kissed you, and I don't think you were faking anything when you kissed me back."

He watched her weigh his words and come to a decision to believe him, to trust her own feelings.

"Couldn't a stallion have got to your mare before or after she was bred to Apollo's Ice?" she asked.

A reasonable question. Maybe it was better to get the factual information over with before dealing with emotions. But they would have to deal with them at some point. He didn't intend to let her push him out of her life without a fight.

"If we were talking about pasture animals," he argued, "of course it would be possible. But we're not. We're talking about prize-winning premium Thoroughbreds whose every grain of food is scrutinized. If a stallion had somehow gotten in with a mare, believe me, we'd know about it."

She conceded his point with a simple nod.

"There's something else," he said. "Some months ago Millions to Spare, a Thoroughbred racehorse owned by Lord Rochester, died under mysterious circumstances in Dubai. Millions to Spare was reputedly sired by Apollo's Ice, as well, but DNA testing subsequently disclosed he was the offspring of the same unknown stallion as our Leopold's Legacy."

Worry furrowed her brow.

"We're not talking about a onetime accident, Devon. We're talking about something much more, a pattern of deceit."

"A conspiracy," she muttered.

He nodded.

"Have other foals of Apollo's Ice been tested?"

"Some of them, and they've proved to be his. But there are more out there, and as yet we don't know how many of them might be imposters."

Her frown deepened. "You're jumping to the conclusion that my brother is behind all this."

"He's the only one with something to gain, Devon. Could someone else be responsible? I suppose so, but to what end? Your brother is the only one who profits by Apollo's Ice producing the maximum number of live foals. Under optimum conditions he can earn anywhere from one to two million dollars in a breeding season."

"That much?" Her brows rose. "I had no idea. Seems like he's always crying poor… But you said these horses are pampered. So how was this stud substitution done?"

"I've thought a lot about that," Brent answered. "I figure there are two ways. One would be to substitute a look-alike for Apollo's Ice."

"Why?"

Brent shrugged. "Horses are quirky animals, as I'm sure you know. They can be a vision of grace and beauty, but they can also be incredibly accident prone. Apollo's Ice might have been injured just before he was supposed to be transported for breeding. Maybe he had an infection of some sort and couldn't pass the vet inspection so he was unsuitable for breeding. Or he could have become

simply have been
sperm count,
ation. There

sterile for some rea
overbred and wa
which would h
are any num asked.
"But uld
"B
all
th

nderstand using a look-alik
able. But if he was available, why
on?"

are pregnant on the first try saves
gives Apollo's Ice a good repu-
ct for a breeding, you're guaran-
hat can stand and nurse. Anything
rocess has to be repeated, which
he mare at the stud farm—at con-
bringing it back the next breeding
derable expense. I've done some
success rate for a single breeding
rcent. That means that almost half
esn't get pregnant or doesn't stay
try. The onetime impregnation rate
se to eighty percent. That's very ap-
ner."

," Devon said.

ventured, "that in addition to mares
pollo's Ice, they were also AI'd in
s fertility statistics. We know, for
ed a foal by the name of Picture of

be taking a mighty big
tive is that artificial ins
probably know, Thorough
by AI. That doesn't mean
breeds permit it, and ther
ring it. For example, ther
the mare or the stallion w
pound animals mounting
registered Thoroughbred
old-fashioned way."

She nodded. "I can u
Apollo's Ice was unavail
use artificial inseminatic

"Because getting a m
mare owners money an
ation. When you contr
ed a live foal—a foal
short of that and the p
means either keeping t
siderable expense—or
season, also at consi
research. The standar
is a little over fifty pe
the time, the mare do
pregnant on the first
for Apollo's Ice is clo
pealing to a mare ow

"I still don't get i
"I think," Brent
being covered by A
order to increase h
example, that he si

Perfection during the same mating season as Leopold's Legacy, and that he covered that mare only once."

Just then a cell phone chirped, interrupting his explanation.

Eight

Devon instantly recognized the ring as hers. Shaking her head in tacit apology for the interruption, she reached for her handbag, which she'd placed on the end table, and took out the phone. The number on display wasn't her mother's or the doctor's, so at least she felt relief that nothing had happened at home. She didn't recognize the series of digits she saw and no name appeared, so she was tempted to ignore it. Instead, she flipped it open and held it to her ear. "Hello."

"Did you think because he's a bloody foreigner I wouldn't know about him?" The deep male voice was raised and angry.

She let out an involuntary gasp, held the phone away from her ear and sprang to her feet.

"I told you to stay away from other men, and I meant it."

"But—"

held her hands for several minutes, and
d expanse of time her emotions rode a
ne moment she was buoyed by the warmth
and the strength seeping into her from him.
was rocked by helplessness and ashamed for
support.

u explain to me what's going on?" he asked,
inuing to clasp her fingers.

ain at first, then with growing confidence and
g anger, she told him about Charles Robinett,
is proposal two years ago, which she'd turned
and finally about his threat against any man who
befriend her.

hat's who was on the phone?"

he nodded and hung her head for a moment, morti-
d by her own weakness. When she looked up, however,
was with fresh determination.

"That's why you must leave, Brent. Immediately.
Charles knows who you are and that we've been to
gether." It sounded so intimate. *Been together.* He'd kissed
her and she wanted him to kiss her again. She wanted
them to *be together* much more intimately. "I can't take
a chance on his following through with his threat, not
against you—"

"Don't worry about me. I can take care of myself."

Of that she had no doubt. In fact, the thought of the two
men clashing held a certain primitive appeal.

"Or against the girls," she added.

"He threatened my children?" His voice was indignant,
uncompromisingly demanding.

"Not specifically, but he knows they're here. I can't
predict what he might do."

"Send him packing or he'll be sorry."

"I—"

"And so will you."

"You can't—"

"I know who he is, Devon. Don't think you can hide
anything from me, because you can't."

"You have no—"

"And I know where to find him and his sweet young
daughters."

"You wouldn't dare— "

"Stay clear of him."

The caller clicked off. She was left standing there
shaking.

"Who was that?" Brent asked, clearly concerned. "Was
that Nolan?"

"No," she said slowly and in little more than a whisper.
She folded the instrument mechanically and let it drop
from the tips of her fingers into her bag.

"Devon, who was that? What did he say?"

"How do you know it was a man?"

"I could hear enough to figure that much." He reached
out to touch her. She flinched, as if she'd received an
electric shock. Startled at her reaction, Brent pulled back.
"What did he say, Devon? Why are you so upset?" This
time when he softly bracketed her shoulders, she didn't
recoil. "You're trembling," he said in alarm.

"It's…nothing."

Brent wrapped his arms protectively around her. She
was so grateful for the comfort of his solid strength she
instinctively relaxed in his embrace.

"Tell me what's going on," he implored against her ear.
"Let me help."

"A crank call," she mumbled. "Nothing to worry about. I'm fine now."

He held her away just enough to look into her eyes. What she found in his was genuine concern, a sincere desire to help her. But what could he do? He was a stranger, a foreigner, and in a few days he would be gone. She felt overwhelmed with loneliness, with helplessness.

"Devon," he pleaded in a solicitous tone, "you're not all right. You're shaking like a leaf."

"Really. It's nothing." She should yank herself away to prove it, but she didn't. "I've had them before. Unnerving, that's all."

She could tell by his expression and the concern in his beautiful blue eyes that he didn't believe her, which should have upset her more, but the result was just the opposite. Knowing he cared made her feel warm inside. It had been so long since a man had held her that way…if ever. What she experienced with Brent…felt for him…was something she'd never encountered before but had dreamed of for so long.

"That was more than a crank call, Devon. A crank call would make you angry. The one you just received has you rattled with fear. Please tell me what's going on."

She forced herself to pull out of his protective embrace. Heather was right. It was time for her to take control of her life, to stand on her own two feet, to stand up to Charles, not cower under his heel. But how? She couldn't depend on Brent to help. He would be leaving soon and returning to America, and she would be left to fight her battles alone.

"I think you ought to go home," she declared firmly.

"What?"

Nearly stumbli… corner where …

"I think you… up your daughter… family and go back…

He stared at her, b… see that, insults or not,… her walk out—without de…

Well, she owed him noth… shoulders, she slipped her … gathered up her purse. As she n… door, he stepped in front of her, hi… on his hips. A colossus.

"Let me go, Brent." She felt so weary,…

"I'm not stopping you, Devon," he s… have to walk around me."

That left her precious little room. It woul… sible to get by this imposing male figure, standin… resolute, without coming into physical contact wi… without brushing against him. She wanted to touch… in the worst sort of way, soak in the heat and power… emanated, but the realization that as soon as she did sh… would have to break contact, that she would be alone once more, nearly smothered her.

She heaved a disheartened sigh and let her stiff, upraised shoulders fall in defeat.

An eternity passed with no sound in the room, save her heart pounding in her ears.

Then she let out a sob and covered her face with her hands. Wordlessly he helped her out of her coat again, tossed it on the back of the chair where she had been sitting and pulled her down onto the love seat beside him.

Brent gazed at her and she could see his outrage, and lurking behind it that wonderful mixture of protective concern and resolve she'd beheld when he'd comforted his daughter. If only she had his strength.

"Don't underestimate him, Brent. He doesn't care whom he uses or whom he hurts to get his way."

"You're right about one thing," he said. "I won't put the welfare of my daughters in jeopardy. But there are a couple of things you ought to know about me. First, I won't be intimidated, and second, once I make up my mind to do something, I refuse to be distracted. I came to England to find out all I can about Apollo's Ice, and I don't intend to leave until I know exactly what's going on. As for threats, real or implied, against me or my family, both you and Charles Robinett need to know I don't take them lightly."

She bowed her head, not in rejection of his bravado or depression over its futility, but in a gentle prayer that he would succeed in his pursuit.

"Surely," Brent went on, "you've told your brother about Charles. What did he say?"

Depression settled over her once more.

"Nolan didn't believe me. He thought I was stupidly misinterpreting Charles's concern for me as a threat and that I was foolish to pass up the opportunities he was offering me as his wife."

Brent stared at her. "What? But you're his sister. Doesn't your happiness count?"

She snorted derisively. "You have to understand something about Nolan. He and Charles are friends, and he refuses to believe Charles would say or do anything... untoward."

"Untoward?" Brent barked. "Perhaps you attach a different meaning to that word on this side of the Atlantic, Devon, but where I come from, untoward is something inconvenient, in poor taste. My God, Charles threatened you."

It struck her immediately that Brent hadn't qualified his statement. He hadn't said *from what you've told me* or *if what you say is true*. He'd accepted her account of the threat unconditionally. Even her own brother hadn't done that.

"Nolan is a bit…status conscious," she said with dry humor. "Charles is a duke. That's several rungs higher in the social pecking order than a viscount."

"And that matters?" Brent regarded her with sudden distaste. "Tell me, do you believe that crap, that fancy titles make people different? Should I start addressing you as Lady Kestler, milady?"

The sarcasm and disdain with which he used the title felt like a slap. She straightened up and pressed her hands against his chest to free herself from his embrace.

"That they make people different, no," she shot back. "That they make a difference in how people who possess them are regarded and treated, yes. You may not have a titled aristocracy in your country, Brent, but you still have the rich and famous, movie stars and politicians."

He had the good grace to smile at the humor in her remark. "Point taken."

They fell silent for several minutes, each cocooned in private thoughts.

"Your brother refuses to believe you're being stalked," Brent finally said, seemingly more angry than before. "He refused to stand up for you and protect you, yet you insist he couldn't possibly be involved in a scheme that could have earned him millions of dollars. That doesn't make sense, Devon."

She opened her mouth to argue, but he wouldn't give her a chance.

"I'm not saying the one is proof of the other, that because he's failed to protect you he's also a fraud. It could be he's just a coward."

"He's not," she protested. *At least he didn't used to be.*

"He's certainly acting like one. I know it doesn't prove he cheated me and Quest Stables, but you have to admit the possibility is strong. If he can let you down when you, his own sister, need his protection, he's also capable of cheating other people, strangers."

He has changed over the past few years, she thought. *I don't know why. I always felt I could depend on him in the past, until Charles came along.*

"How did he and Charles meet?" Brent asked, as if he had been reading her mind. "In school?"

She paced toward the window, heard the rain that had begun to fall drumming softly against the panes.

"Nolan is five years older than Charles," she said, "so they weren't in school at the same time. They met at a race, I think, or maybe at a social event following one."

"Does Charles own horses?"

"I don't think so. He spends a good deal of time at various tracks, though, and I've heard he's been involved in a few inquiries concerning fixed races, but he has influential friends, so--"

"Nothing's ever come of it," Brent finished for her.

She glanced away disconsolately. The rain was coming down harder. The sound of it made the room feel smaller, more isolated, more intimate.

"Maybe I can find something on the Internet," Brent said, "now that I have a better idea of what I'm looking for. Is that his full name, Charles Robinett?"

She nodded.

"You said he's a duke. Doesn't that mean he has a title? What is it?"

"He's the Duke of Camberg."

Watching Devon leave that night had been more difficult than Brent would ever have expected. It had happened again, just as it had with Marti. One encounter and all his male instincts were ganging up on him. With Marti it had been the power of her laugh, her joy in living, as well as her beauty and charm. With Devon it was her vulnerability that appealed to his protective instincts.

For better or for worse, he was bound to this young woman. He hoped Marti would understand. Perhaps when the case was solved his attraction to Devon would be over, as well. In the meantime he couldn't let it interfere with what he had to do. This past year had been one of guilt and regrets, and it was far from over. His regrets now encompassed their kiss, not because it had happened, but because he'd never gotten a chance to pursue it further. She'd kissed him back in a way that spoke of a need and hunger that paralleled his own.

The regret he felt for misleading his daughters, however, was laced with guilt. He should have been more sensitive to their vulnerabilities.

What he felt about Devon's situation with Charles Robinett, however, was neither regret nor guilt as much as moral outrage that any man would victimize a woman as he had, particularly that he would punish—no, torment—Devon to such an extent.

London's six-hour time difference with Kentucky was to his advantage, Brent realized as he picked up the phone. It was 10 p.m. in England, but only late afternoon in the Bluegrass State. Devon had left only minutes earlier. Unhappy. And he had been part of the reason. But he'd also sensed a mood of determination he hadn't witnessed before. He had provided her with several shockers tonight. That her brother might be involved in fraudulent activities, activities that could threaten his freedom as well as his reputation. And then there was the news that she had an illegitimate half brother.

He dialed his older brother's cell phone number, which was picked up on the third ring.

"Are you making any progress?" Andrew asked, after the usual exchange of greetings.

"I've found out who Camberg is," Brent told him. "His name is Charles Robinett. He's the Duke of Camberg, a pal of Nolan's. He's also been stalking Nolan's sister, Devon."

"Nice pal."

Brent recounted the situation as Devon had described it. The brothers agreed that a man who wouldn't protect his own sister was beneath contempt.

"I'm more convinced than ever that Nolan's behind this mess. I have a problem, though," Brent went on. "I screwed up royally with the girls."

He told Andrew about his visit with the twins to the girls' academy and Katie's fear that they were going to be left there, abandoned. Even now, Brent felt sick inside. After all the girls had been through, losing their mother and moving in with their grandparents, it was totally insensitive for him to bring them to a place where other children were treated as castoffs.

"The poor kids," Andrew commiserated.

"Under the circumstances it's not safe to have them here with me, though. I've thought about bringing them home, then coming back, but I've been wondering if maybe Mom and Dad could come over and stay with them. That way they'll feel secure, I'll be free to come and go and will know they're completely safe. Do you think they might be willing to do that?"

"I can ask them, Brent, but I really don't have to. We both know what the answer will be. The only question is how soon they can get a flight."

Brent let out a pent-up breath. "We're spending tonight in Oxford, but we'll be returning by train to London in the morning." He gave the name of the hotel they were staying at.

"Got it. I'll call you and let you know when they'll be arriving at Heathrow."

Nine

Devon was bubbly with the girls the following morning when they all met for breakfast at the Sword and Shield. Brent wasn't fooled, however. Behind the laughter and quips he spied confusion and unhappiness. He doubted she'd slept much the previous night. If the vicious call from Charles hadn't been enough to shake her up, Brent's revelation that she had a half brother would have preoccupied her mind. And now, in addition to all those worries, she had to seriously question whether her brother might be involved in something far more sinister— criminal activity that could bring shame to the family.

"I have good news," he told the twins, after they had settled down with their bangers and eggs. "A surprise."

Katie seemed to have recovered from her anxiety attack of the night before, but he wondered what was going through her mind, if deep down inside she was still afraid. The thought that he had brought on this insecurity still tormented him. He wondered if what he was about to tell them would improve the situation or make it worse. Once again he was tempted to announce they were returning home, then wait a while before coming back by himself.

There were problems with that plan, too. Quest's financial situation was getting worse. Cash reserves, substantial as they were, thanks to Andrew's sound management, were quickly being depleted. Unless this mess could be straightened out soon, Quest would have to close completely. There was even the possibility that the land would have to be sold. Their grandfather was eighty-six years old. His health was remarkably good, but even the old iron horse wouldn't live forever. Brent couldn't bear the thought of Hugh going to his grave with his legacy in ruins.

The other impediment to his returning home was Devon. Knowing what he did, he could no more board a plane and desert her than he could dump the twins off at a boarding school. Some people might say he owed her nothing, even that her situation was none of his business.

Except that he had kissed her. There were still many things he wanted to know about her, but she was not a stranger to him. In the years since Marti's death, he hadn't looked at another woman, hadn't touched another woman. But he had looked at Devon. He had touched her. He had kissed her lips and felt her respond to him.

The three females at the table were staring at him.

"What's the surprise, Daddy?" Rhea asked him impatiently.

"I talked to Uncle Andrew last evening on the phone, and guess what? Grandma and Grandpa are coming over to be with us."

"They are?" Katie asked. Brent could see the shadow of suspicion in her clear blue eyes.

"Yep. They decided they needed a vacation, too. They're flying in this afternoon."

Devon studied him with uncertainty. "What time are they arriving?"

"They get into Heathrow at four this afternoon. I figure if we get the ten-eighteen train to London from here, we'll have more than enough time to drop off our luggage, grab a bite to eat, then go to the airport to meet them."

Devon merely nodded. She said nothing until after they left the hotel and were on their way to the doll shop. The girls were skipping ahead of them, holding hands.

Brent found it inspirational and reached for Devon's. She seemed reluctant at first, but then she folded her hand into his and squeezed.

"Why are your parents coming over?" she asked a moment later.

"After what Katie said last night, I decided they needed to feel more secure. They're close to my parents."

"Is that all?" Her tone wasn't accusatory, but Brent didn't miss the note of suspicion in it.

"I need to do more investigating. I thought I could do it with them in tow, but after learning about your brother's friend last night, I can't take the chance of putting them in danger. My folks will protect them while giving me the freedom I need."

"You could just go home?"

He stopped and turned to her, still holding her hand. "I won't abandon you, Devon."

"And if I tell you I don't want you to stay, that I don't need you to play Lord Protector for me—"

"Is this a test?" he asked with a smile on his face, a smile he knew had to be crooked because he felt no joy or humor in her question. "If I say I'll stay anyway, you can accuse me of being as overbearing as Charles. If I say I'll go, you can criticize me for leaving you in the lurch, like your brother. Either way I can't win, can I?"

She lowered her head.

He tipped it up and stared into her brown eyes. "Either way, you lose, too, Devon. I care for you. I'm willing to do whatever it takes to help and protect you. Call me Don Quixote, if you like, but I will never force myself on you. You need to know that."

She bit her lip and broke eye contact. "Thank you," she murmured.

"Come on, Daddy. What are you waiting for?" Rhea called and impatiently waved for them to join Katie and her.

They all entered the doll shop together.

"Oh, aren't these lovely," Devon exclaimed, as she scanned the rows of dolls, each face hand painted and unique, each dress hand sewn and distinctive.

"I like that one," Rhea called out, "the red one with the gold stuff."

Devon chuckled, while the shopkeeper cringed slightly. "Stuff" apparently wasn't a preferred term for the delicate gold ribbon trim on the doll's billowy crimson gown.

"I like the blue one better," Katie said, pointing to a

slightly smaller doll in a soft sky-blue gown, accented with white lace and a broad-brimmed hat of the same fine filigree.

"Or maybe that one," Rhea muttered, pointing to another doll, this one in purple and red. She preferred bold colors and contrasts, while her sister was drawn to more subtle combinations.

The girls changed their minds half a dozen times over the course of the next thirty minutes.

"You're going to miss your train," Devon reminded Brent.

"That's all right. There's another one in an hour. We have more than enough time to get to Heathrow."

Brent stood back and smiled contentedly as his daughters discussed their likes and dislikes with Devon, constantly asking her opinion, though they sometimes disagreed with it. There was a lot of giggling, too. About the time Brent was beginning to feel left out, Devon would look over at him and wink. They left the shop nearly an hour after they'd entered. By then, the girls had come full circle and settled on the first two dolls they'd fallen in love with.

They were walking back to the hotel to collect their luggage and get a taxi to the train station, when Devon reached out and clasped Brent's hand. The gesture pleased him enormously, but he also sensed a kind of desperation in it, as if she were grasping for a lifeline. Maybe she was. For that matter, maybe he was, too.

"I didn't sleep much last night," she confessed as the girls ran ahead toward the hotel.

"I'm not surprised. I dumped an awful lot on you. I'm sorry."

"It's not your fault. Well—" she tried to smile to

lighten her somber mood "—maybe it is. If you hadn't told me all those things—"

There were other things he would have preferred talking about, like their kiss. That alone had had the power to keep him awake in his bed, but mentioning it now would have complicated things for both of them.

He clutched her hand with his free one. In the other he carried the shiny shopping bag containing the two porcelain dolls.

"Would you rather not have known?" he asked.

"A part of me says yes." They walked on in silence for a minute. "You're convinced all those things you told me are true, aren't you?"

"I don't go around telling people lies, Devon."

She glanced up at him, one brow raised, almost in amusement. He felt unaccustomed heat suffuse his face. Even that statement was technically a lie.

"Not about things that really matter." He tightened his grip on her hand.

Her lips curled at the edges. The corners of her eyes crinkled with humor. Then she grew sober again. "No," she said with a sigh, "I don't suppose you do."

"But you still don't believe me."

"I don't want to believe you, Brent. What's so troubling, what kept me awake most of the night, is that I don't know if I do or not. A few years ago there was no possibility I'd give credence to charges that made my brother anything less than a good and honorable man."

"And then Charles—"

She raised her free hand, as if to wave the subject, the bitter memory, away.

"I went to him about Charles and saw a side of Nolan

I'd never known existed. I don't want to believe what you've told me now—"

"But there's doubt."

"There's doubt," she acknowledged bitterly, angrily. "Some of what you said rang too true." After a pause, she continued. "My father was not a pleasant man to live with, Brent. He was a tyrant and a bully. That he impregnated some poor woman and then walked away without a backward glance doesn't surprise me. God knows how many other Hunter bastards are running around out there." She stopped. "I'm sorry. I shouldn't be talking this way. It's unkind and unfair. As for this Marcus Vasquez you mentioned, he was better off growing up without a father than with Nigel Hunter."

"I'm sorry he hurt you," Brent said.

She didn't hear pity in his words, only sympathy, and that meant the world to her. Maybe it was Hunter vanity coming through, but she hated the thought of being pitied.

"I believed my brother was different," she went on. "He used to be. When I was young, he was the big brother I could always run to when my father was in a rage. And Nolan never let me down. Then something changed." She paused. "In Charles I saw my father's vices rather than my brother's virtue, so I rejected him. But it seems Nolan's association with Charles has brought out my father's vices in him, as well."

She grew introspective for a moment. "I love my mother, but I can't deny that she's weak, not just in the physical sense. Maybe she had to be like that to get on with my father. I'm not judging her. I'm only saying I don't want a life like hers. I'd rather be alone than live in someone else's shadow, always afraid."

Ten

watch Hall, overlooking Hyde Park, was not parly impressive from the outside: four stories of agekened brown brick with evenly spaced black-shuttered ndows. The shiny, red front door was flanked by two white marble Greek columns. The only ostentation, if one could call it that, was the polished brass door knocker in the form of a roaring lion.

"Is this your house?" Rhea asked.

"This is where I grew up," Devon replied. "We have a country place in Abbingvale, just outside of Cambridge, where we went every summer, but most of the time we lived here."

"Do I detect irony?" Brent asked, as they mounted the three steps to the front door. "You lived in Cambridge and now work in Oxford."

Brent squeezed her hand. "You're strong, Devon."

"I haven't been till now. I've been exactly what I said I don't want to be, someone who cowers under another person's power."

She put up her hand to forestall his comment. "I've decided to go with you, Brent, to London."

"To London?" Brent felt like an idiot repeating her words. At the same time he couldn't help imagining them walking hand in hand, as they were doing now, through Hyde Park, along the Thames, ducking into doorways during cloudbursts, kissing while they waited for the storm to pass.

"The girls will be glad to hear that," he said, "and so am I. But why, Devon? Why?"

"To face my demons," she said with a kind of introspective resoluteness. She paused and looked up at him. "No, to fight them. I don't know if the things you told me last night are true, if my brother is as dishonest as you make him out to be. I admit he's become a disappointment to me, but that's not the same, is it? Now I have to find out for myself."

"But what about school? Your job?"

"I'll call Mrs. Sherwood-Griffin this afternoon and explain that a family matter has arisen. She knows my mother's health is precarious—"

"You'll lie to her?"

She flushed, then remembered her new resolve. "If I have to. I've been training a new assistant. She can take over. She's quite competent actually, and the children like her."

"Good." He brought her hand up against his chest, pressed it there as he gazed into her sad eyes. "You don't

want your br
though I
you, I'
an
I wo

"I k
together

"Very perceptive, Mr. Preston," she said with mocking formality. "One that's been remarked on before."

"Oops." He staggered back dramatically. "I seem to have tripped on a cliché."

She laughed.

"Daddy, you didn't trip on anything," Katie said. "I saw you."

He laughed, too. "It's a figure of speech, honey."

The girls looked at each other and shrugged, while Devon removed a key from her purse. Before she could insert it, however, the door was opened from the inside by a man in his late fifties wearing a morning coat and striped gray trousers.

"Good morning, Miss Hunter," he said.

"Hello, Perkins." She ushered the girls in ahead of her, then entered herself.

"Perkins," she said, when Brent was across the threshold, "this is Mr. Brent Preston and his daughters, Rhea and Katie. I'll let you try to sort them out. I'm still not sure who is who myself. They're from Kentucky in America."

The butler bowed his head slightly in greeting. "Welcome to London, Mr. Preston."

Brent thanked him and "sorted out" his two daughters. "They've promised to be on their best behavior," he intimated behind his hand.

"No, we didn't, Daddy," Katie spoke up.

Almost imperceptibly, Perkins pulled in his cheeks, the tiniest hint of a smile playing on his lips.

Brent raised his right eyebrow. "But you will be, won't you?"

The two bobbed their heads in unison. "Of course we will, Daddy," Rhea said sweetly.

"Sure, Daddy," Katie agreed.

"I knew I could count on the two of you. My sweet little angels."

The girls tittered.

Devon chuckled. The easy, unselfconscious rapport among them was heartwarming.

"Lady Kestler is in the drawing room, miss."

"Thank you, Perkins."

"Luncheon is available at your convenience."

"Perfect." She turned to Brent and the girls. "Let's go see Mother."

The girls craned their necks at the marble entranceway with its crystal chandelier and Louis Quatorze gilded furniture. They bumped into each other as they followed Devon down the hall and into a room on the right.

A chubby woman with silver-gray hair, every strand rigidly in place, sat in a motorized wheelchair near a large fireplace of carved cream-colored marble. Lady Kestler wore a calf-length pink lace dress and white buckled shoes, an outfit that Brent found oddly inappropriate for a matriarch. He couldn't imagine his own mother wearing such getup. It seemed more suited to a bridesmaid.

She had oxygen prongs in her nose from a small tank affixed to the back of her chair. Brent knew she was not yet sixty-five, but as he drew closer he realized that despite the plumpness of her skin and carefully applied cosmetics, she looked much older.

Putting aside the small volume in her gnarled hands, she opened her arms to Devon, who bent and kissed her on the cheek.

"Mother, may I present Mr. Brent Preston from the United States? My mother, Sarah, the Viscountess Kestler."

The elderly woman looked up and extended her right hand, palm down. "Mr. Preston, I'm delighted to meet you."

Brent took her hand gently in his, not sure if he was expected to bend and kiss it. He really must check on the customs here.

"Lady Kestler, I'm very pleased to meet you. May I present my children—" he waved to the girls "—Rhea and Katie."

Brent wasn't surprised that they were intimidated by the setting, if not the woman herself. He was grateful, however, that their shyness resulted in silence.

"Hi," Rhea said first with a little wave of her hand.

Katie followed her sister's lead. "Yeah, hi."

"Hi," Lady Kestler returned with a twinkle in her hazel eyes. "Please do sit down, all of you," she invited them, and proceeded smoothly to engage the girls in small talk, asking where they had been and what they'd seen.

When Devon announced to the girls that she was coming to London with them and that her mother had invited them to luncheon at her town house, Brent had persuaded them to change from their brightly colored pants to more conservative dresses. They'd balked initially but had finally complied. Now he was glad they had. They would have been overdressed for Winipy's, but not in this setting. He suspected they were aware of it, too.

"How long will you be staying in England, Mr. Preston?" Lady Kestler asked him.

"I'm not sure. Probably for a couple of weeks."

"Then it's back to Kentucky? I understand you raise horses there, and that you know my son, Nolan."

"Yes, ma'am. We met here in London several months ago for the first time and again in Florida over the New Year."

"Then you've seen him more recently than I," she noted. Her disappointment—maybe even her bitterness—was in the words rather than the delivery. "The boy is forever on the move."

The boy she was referring to was thirty-five years old. Did Brent's mother refer to her sons as boys? He was surprised to realize she often did. To a mother, he supposed, a son was always a boy.

"Brent's sister is a jockey," Devon said, "and beat Nolan's horse at the Gulf Classic."

"How fascinating. Have you seen him on this trip?"

"No, ma'am. Not yet. I'm hoping to meet him and Charles Robinett while I'm here."

"Camberg?" she asked, her lips subtly thinning. Brent wondered what reason she might have for disliking the man, since Devon said she'd never discussed his threats with her mother.

"I understand he's interested in racing," Brent remarked casually. "I thought we might compare notes."

"You must join us then at Morningfield Manor next weekend for the Archers' Ball. He'll be there, and you can visit our stables."

"That's very kind of you." Brent glanced quickly at Devon. "I look forward to it."

"My late husband started the winter ball more than thirty years ago," Lady Kestler explained with a note of pride. "We've continued it, of course."

Brent nodded. "I'm honored to be invited."

Lady Kestler led them to a cozy morning room overlooking a well-tended winter conservatory at the back of the house for lunch. The formal dining room, he was told, was upstairs on the first floor.

"When Devon told me you were coming here I tried to think of something that might appeal to the girls. Devon and Nolan always enjoyed Toad in a Hole."

Eyes wide and mouth hanging open with a look of horror, Katie tugged on her father's sleeve as Devon walked beside her mother's chair ahead of them.

"Daddy," she said in a nervous whisper, "I don't want to eat a toad."

"Me, neither," Rhea added. "Oh, yuck."

He stopped them by placing his hands on their shoulders and bending toward them. "You don't even know what it is. It might be something you really like."

Their faces lit up with relief. "It isn't a toad then?" Katie asked.

"What's a corn dog?"

"That's silly, Daddy. A corn dog is a hot dog inside corn bread."

"Is a hot dog made of dog?"

"Daddy!" Both girls glared at him in outraged shock at the very idea.

He laughed.

They arrived at the morning room.

"What's so funny?" Devon asked him, as they were being seated.

"The girls want to know what Toad in a Hole is. We don't have anything by that name back home."

She smiled. "You like bangers, don't you?" she asked the girls.

"They're good," Katie said.

"And you like Yorkshire pudding?"

"That's my favorite," Rhea declared.

"Well, that's what Toad in a Hole is. Yorkshire pudding with bangers baked in it."

"Mmm," both girls agreed.

"And for dessert," Lady Kestler announced, "we'll be having frog spawn."

Eleven

Frog spawn turned out to be tapioca pudding, which, though not one of the girls' favorites, was less objectionable than its name, and Brent was proud of them when they ate it without complaining, gagging, retching or making unpleasant remarks.

Following the leisurely lunch, Lady Kestler excused herself to retire to her room upstairs for a rest. By then it was time to go to Heathrow to meet Brent's parents.

Because of security and customs inspection, Brent and his daughters were not allowed to go to the gate to greet the senior Prestons, so they all waited anxiously behind the incoming checkpoint for them.

"You'd think they hadn't seen their grandparents in months instead of only days," Brent said quietly in Devon's ear. She caught the musky scent of his aftershave.

The girls anxiously peered down the long concourse, as incoming passengers streamed by.

Devon wished she could tell him how much she envied their closeness. She couldn't remember ever being so keyed up at the prospect of joining her family. As much as she loved her mother, even being reunited with her at holidays when she came home from boarding school wasn't this emotionally exciting.

"Why don't I hold those for you," Devon said to the girls, as she reached for their dolls.

They'd insisted on bringing them, even though their father had strongly suggested it would be better to leave them at the hotel. Devon would never have challenged her own father on such a matter, nor would she have had a chance of changing his mind.

Without offering much resistance, both girls now gave up the dolls that were more collector's items than toys.

"There they are." Brent pointed to a middle-aged couple approaching with small pieces of hand luggage.

"Where? Where?" The girls bounced up, trying to see.

Devon took only a moment to spy Brent's parents, who had started waving and rushing forward through the throng. His mother, she noted, was slender and strikingly attractive, even in casual traveling clothes. His father, tall, large framed and distinguished-looking, was in many ways an older version of Brent himself. He had the same thick, dark brown hair, though the senior Preston was graying at the temples.

The fatigue Devon had initially recognized in his parents' plodding strides had instantly vanished the moment they saw their son and granddaughters. Once past the electronic gates, they threw themselves into hugs and kisses, first with the children, then with their son, who didn't hesitate to return the affection.

Brent introduced Devon to his parents as Miss Devon Hunter.

"It's just Devon," she said, extending her hand to Jenna. "I'm so very pleased to meet you, Mr. Preston. I hope your flight was uneventful," she added as she took Thomas Preston's hand.

"A mark of our times," Brent's father said, "that we prefer boredom to activity."

"We came in her mother's car," Rhea shouted. "She calls it a saloon."

"Isn't that silly, calling a car a barroom?" Katie added.

"I think Devon means it's like a living room," Jenna explained, then turned to look at her son. "I won't ask where my granddaughter learned about barrooms," she commented wryly.

"We have a driver, too," Katie said. "But that's all right, 'cause he knows how to drive on the wrong side of the street."

"I think tomorrow some tutoring in diplomacy and foreign relations may be in order," Jenna said with a happy chuckle. The adults all laughed as they departed the building.

"You have absolutely wonderful grandchildren, Mrs. Preston," Devon told her. "I wouldn't want to change a thing."

"They are wonderful, aren't they?" the older woman agreed. "Brent turned out pretty well, too, don't you agree? And please call me Jenna."

On the way into town, Brent asked about his grandfather.

"He's fine," Thomas assured him. "I know you worry

about him, Brent, but don't. He's tough. He's been through a lot in his lifetime."

"That's why this is all so unfair. He's got to be discouraged at this point." Brent was tempted to add "and disappointed with me," but he didn't want it to sound like this was about him. It was about Quest Stables and Hugh Preston's legacy. "I wish, after all these months, I could tell him I'm closer to resolving the problem."

"You are, son," Thomas told him without a hint of recrimination. "You just don't realize it yet. You've eliminated a mountain of possibilities and suspects. That narrows the trail."

"Was it Sherlock Holmes," Jenna remarked, "or Hercule Poirot who said when you have eliminated everything else, what's left must be the answer."

"Depends on the accent, Mom," Brent said with a chuckle. "If he sounded like Devon, it was Sherlock. If he sounded like Maurice Chevalier, it was Hercule."

"Smart aleck." Jenna laughed.

"Who's Maurice Chevalier?" Devon asked.

The two older people stared at her, until Brent snickered. Then they all burst out laughing.

"Gotcha," Brent said, and impulsively gave Devon a peck on the cheek. Her slight blush made him feel unimaginably lighthearted. He didn't miss the expression of surprise that passed between his parents. His impulsive act caught them off guard, but he was relieved to realize it didn't earn their disapproval.

Leaning back into the plush upholstery of the luxury sedan, he also appreciated his father's earlier vote of confidence and encouragement. But until the mystery of

Leopold's Legacy was solved and the family could reclaim their proud name, none of it counted for much.

They arrived at the hotel. The doorman opened the passenger door.

Brent had been able to reserve the suite across the hall from him and the girls for his parents. They got settled in within a matter of minutes.

"I suppose it's too late for one of your lovely English teas," Jenna commented to Devon after putting the last of her toiletries away.

Devon winked at Brent. "Not for some people, it isn't. Would you like to have it here or in the dining room downstairs?"

"Can we have biscuits and cream?" Katie asked Devon.

"She means scones and clotted cream," Brent clarified.

"Up here, I think," Jenna said. "That way we can talk."

Devon picked up the phone on the writing table between the windows overlooking the park and pressed a button.

"This is Miss Hunter. Lady Kestler would like to order tea for four adults and two children, please. Yes, the usual selection. That will be quite satisfactory. Thank you." She replaced the receiver. "It'll be about twenty minutes."

Brent came over to her, cocked his head to one side and nodded theatrically. "I stand corrected, milady. Titles do make a difference."

She laughed. "I don't think Mother would object to my using her name. Besides, you haven't seen the bill yet."

In fact, the "tea" was delivered in exactly twenty minutes, and Jenna settled in quite comfortably to play "mother."

Leave it to her, Brent thought, to ask Devon questions he hadn't even thought of.

"Where did you attend primary and secondary school?" Jenna asked.

"I went to boarding school."

"Briar Hills Academy?" Brent asked. It hadn't occurred to him that she might have been an alumna there.

She nodded. "My father went to Oxford, as did my brother. He expected me to go there, as well, but when the time came, I chose Cambridge instead."

"Did that upset him?" Jenna asked.

"He'd passed away by then."

"What did you study there?"

"English and music, specializing in medieval texts."

"What instruments do you play?" Brent asked.

"Piano and violin. Not at the same time, of course."

"Mother plays the piano and Dad is no slouch with a fiddle himself," Brent pointed out.

"Country fiddle," Thomas clarified. "And strictly by ear. I can't read music worth a hoot."

"Which is your favorite?" Jenna asked.

Devon tilted her head thoughtfully. "Depends completely on my mood. Do you play?" she asked Brent.

"Country music, like Dad," he admitted. "Stringed instruments, guitar, banjo, mandolin. None of them very well."

"He's too modest," Jenna said. "Except in this case he's right."

"Gee, thanks, Mom."

She laughed. "And always so serious."

When Devon rose to leave, she apologized for not being able to invite them to Pathwatch Hall for dinner, but explained that her mother wasn't up to entertaining guests twice in one day. She hoped that while the Prestons were visiting they would have an opportunity to meet her.

The girls, who had been remarkably quiet during the adults' conversation, jumped up to protest Devon's leaving and to hug her goodbye.

"I'm sure we'll meet again, and very soon I hope."

After the formalities of farewell, Brent rode with her down to the lobby. The Rolls-Royce was standing by, ready to take her back to her mother's house. They stood in the elevator alcove, out of view of casual passersby. He put his arms around her.

"I'll call you tomorrow and let you know our schedule. When are you planning to go to Morningfield Manor? I'd like to go with you, if that's okay."

"Of course. I want you to. Wednesday morning. Mother won't be coming up until late Thursday. That'll give me time to make sure everything is prepared for her arrival."

He kissed her. She started to object, but then kissed him back, tightening her grip on him.

A minute later he watched as the doorman handed her into the posh black Rolls.

"Have you been able to learn anything more?" Thomas asked his son later that evening in the sitting room of Brent's hotel suite. They were enjoying a nightcap while Jenna put the girls to bed.

"Other than the identity of Camberg," Brent told him, "not really, but as our English hosts would say, it's early days."

"Andrew said this guy Camberg is an English duke."

Brent nodded. "I checked him out on the Internet. He's thirty years old, took the title six years ago after his father was killed in a private plane crash. Attended Eton and King's College, Oxford, where he had a reputation for partying rather than scholarship. Hereditary Camberg title goes back to the Restoration after the English Civil War, along with a large estate in the Midlands. Charles's mother, unlike Lady Kestler, also comes from the aristocracy and is, several generations back, related to the Austrian Hapsburg line in Europe."

"I guess I'm impressed," Thomas said laconically.

"He has two sisters," Brent continued, "both younger, married and living abroad. One in France, the other in Australia."

"What does he do?" Thomas asked.

"Not much of anything, as far as I can tell. His father was apparently a good businessman who managed to increase the family's wealth considerably. Charles seems intent on spending it. He has a reputation as a playboy. Drives expensive sports cars and seems to smash them up regularly. He settled a civil claim against him a couple of years ago by the family of a young man he crippled for life in one of his crashes. Avoided criminal charges, thanks to the efforts of the very high-priced solicitor he hired. Rumor has it he shelled out five million quid to resolve the matter out of court. He likes to play the horses, both flat and steeplechase racing, and from tabloid reports I found online, his name has cropped up in half a dozen inquiries at various tracks. He's been warned off three of them, though nothing has been officially proved, and no formal charges have ever been brought. But then, as Devon has pointed out, the family has considerable influence in certain quarters."

"She's a lovely girl," Jenna commented, coming out of the twins' bedroom and quietly closing the door behind her. "What are you gents drinking? Can I have some?"

"Brent's nursing a brandy. I'm having Scotch," Thomas said, getting up from the love seat and moving over to the drinks table. "Which will it be?"

"Scotch, please." Jenna ensconced herself in the love seat. "Does she know why you're here?"

"It didn't take her very long to figure out we aren't here on vacation—or holiday, as she would phrase it."

"No, I don't imagine it would," Jenna said.

"She strikes me as a very intelligent girl, as well as a pretty one," Thomas said as he handed his wife her drink. He settled on the little sofa beside her.

A perfect picture, it seemed to Brent, his parents sitting side by side, completely at ease in each other's company. He'd had that once with Marti. Now, though, when he thought of sitting beside a woman, close enough to touch, it was Devon who came to mind. The prospect filled him with new hope.

"The two of you seem to have hit it off," Jenna remarked after her first taste of Scotch.

"It's happened so fast," he said, feeling especially guilty, since today was the anniversary of Marti's death.

"It was the same with Marti," Jenna reminded him. "Two magnets pulling toward each other. Irresistible."

Leave it to his mother to read his mind. She'd loved Marti like a daughter, yet she was willing to let her be a part of the past. Thomas was no less accepting of Devon. That meant a great deal to Brent, their permission, their encouragement to move on.

"This whole business must be very difficult for her," Jenna observed.

Brent nodded. "She doesn't want to believe her brother is less than noble, and for her sake I don't want him to be, either. He was her hero, her protector, when their father was alive. But she admits that in the last couple of years he's changed, and not for the better. He refused to stand up for her against Camberg."

When his parents both looked blank, he realized his brother must not have filled them in. He told them about Devon's being stalked by her brother's "friend" and wasn't surprised at their reaction of horror.

"Can you trust her?" Thomas asked a moment later.

It was a reasonable question, one Brent had had to ask himself. After all, her family's name and reputation were on the line.

"Yes," he said bluntly. "She's had to face a pretty harsh world, despite her privilege. From what I can tell, her father was physically abusive on occasion, emotionally cold and uncaring. And then there's Camberg, so she's not naive about the world."

Brent felt his anger start to flare. "I haven't had the pleasure of meeting the gentleman yet, but I will this weekend. I've been invited to attend the annual ball at Morningfield Manor, the Kestler estate in Cambridge-shire."

He paused to take a sip of his brandy. "Devon's main concern at the moment is her mother. Lady Kestler is in fragile health, has been for years. If it turns out her first-born is a liar and a cheat who could end up going to prison, it might be more than the poor woman can handle."

Jenna sipped her whisky. "I haven't met the woman, but I'm willing to bet she's stronger than people give her credit for."

Brent and his father both turned to her.

"Care to elaborate, my dear?" Thomas asked.

Twelve

"You said earlier that Lady Kestler was unaware of Marcus being her husband's illegitimate son." There was a healthy dose of skepticism in Jenna's voice. "I think it's quite probable, however, that she's known about him from the beginning."

"How can you possibly know that?" Brent asked.

"I may be wrong, of course." Jenna took another sip of her drink while the two men waited expectantly.

"Please, don't stop now, Mother."

Jenna studied the glass in her hand for a moment. "My guess is that Lady Kestler knew from the beginning that her husband was a philanderer and an adulterer." She turned to Brent. "You said you researched the family. What did you find?"

"The Hunters lost their estate—it was called Wicker-bale or something like that—and the bulk of their wealth in the early twentieth century. As far as I can tell, it was a result of the Great War, which left many of the hereditary nobility nearly destitute, and in some cases without a male heir."

"And the Morningfields?"

"Gentry. Commoners. Made their fortune in nineteenth-century commerce and bought the estate now called Morningfield Manor in the late 1920s from one of those destitute aristocrats. Not the Kestlers, if that's what you're thinking."

"The irony would be too much, wouldn't it?" Jenna noted. "What about Sarah Morningfield?"

"She had an older unmarried brother who was a pilot in the RAF. Killed in the blitz. Sarah attended Cambridge after the war. The only published picture I found of her was her wedding picture on the society page."

"Let me hazard a guess," Jenna said. "She was…shall we say…plain?"

Brent shrugged nonjudgmentally. "Short and pudgy, from what I could make out. The picture was grainy. All I can tell you is that the woman I met today was very charming and dignified but, honestly, I can't imagine she was ever particularly attractive, certainly no raving beauty."

"And in the wedding picture Nigel Hunter is tall and handsome."

Brent shrugged. "I suppose so. Tall and imposing, at least."

"As well as two years her junior."

"What are you getting at, Mother?" Brent asked, though he thought he knew.

Jenna swirled the single-malt whisky around in her glass. "My guess is that their marriage was one of convenience. Convenient for her because it brought her into the nobility. Opportune for him because it gave him access to the Morningfield fortune."

Brent and his father made eye contact, each lifting their brows and shrugging.

"Makes sense, I suppose," Thomas said. "But what bearing does any of that have on the current situation? The old reprobate's been dead for years."

"Let's suppose," Jenna went on patiently, "for the sake of argument, that Nolan is responsible for this breeding fraud. What would his motive be?"

"Money, of course," Brent said. "What else could it be? Apollo's Ice was bringing in enormous stud fees. By my reckoning, between one and two million dollars a year. Even in British pounds that's a heap of dough."

"But the family has plenty of money. The car Lady Kestler sent to pick us up at the airport was a Rolls-Royce. She lives alone in a London mansion off Hyde Park with a full staff of servants, and has a country house which, according to Devon, is also fully stuffed."

"Okay, she's wealthy," Brent agreed. "That's no secret."

"I think she's wealthy because she never gave up control of the Morningfield fortune."

Brent stared at her, then bowed his head as he gave the statement some consideration. "You're suggesting she had her husband on an allowance and now she has her son on one. That makes her pretty manipulative, Mother."

Yet Brent couldn't completely dismiss the possibility. He thought of the plain matron he'd met, dressed in a manner that would have been too young for a woman half her age. What did that say about her?

"We know Nolan lives well," Jenna went on.

Again, her son nodded. "When I was here last time, I visited him in his London flat. He has expensive tastes."

"He certainly wears fine clothes," she pointed out. "He has a stable of horses, and when he travels he goes first class. Yet he has no regular job."

"He's also the Viscount Kestler," Thomas observed. "Wouldn't he have inherited a bundle from his father along with the title? Isn't it more likely he's controlling the purse strings and maintaining his invalid mother in her lifestyle?"

"You're probably right," Jenna replied, though it was clear she didn't think so. "Still," she mused, "someone who would serve up his sister to the likes of Camberg doesn't strike me as the type of man who would keep his mother in the lap of luxury. Unless he's a mama's boy."

Thomas scoffed. "I don't think so."

"He could be a wily investor," Brent reflected, "but somehow I don't see him in that role, either. Devon, on the other hand, has a job as a teacher and shares an apartment…a flat…with a school colleague. If Lady Kestler is the source of Nolan's disposable cash, why hasn't Devon been equally well provided for?"

Thomas shrugged. "Good questions. Seems to me it's more likely that a mother would provide for her daughter than for an intelligent, able-bodied son."

"As crass as it sounds," Brent muttered, "maybe I ought to ask Devon about money. What are your plans for tomorrow?" he asked, changing the subject. He didn't want to be distracted by thoughts of Devon right now.

"I thought we'd go to a travel agent in the morning," Jenna replied, "and see what's available this time of year. Stratford-upon-Avon, of course. Warwick Castle and Hampton Court are both storybook lovely, even if the girls are too young to fully appreciate their historic significance. I'm sure an agent can come up with others. Maybe a train tour into Scotland. Too bad it's winter. Summer would be better for touring Edinburgh. Still—"

"How long do you want us out of your way?" Thomas asked.

Brent was tempted to say, not at all. He wished he could go with them. He hadn't visited most of those places himself and he loved watching the twins' reactions to new adventures.

"The ball at Morningfield Manor is next weekend," he said, "and Devon says I can travel up there with her on Wednesday, so I'll be around here tomorrow and Tuesday. Maybe we can do a few things together, and still give me time to do more research. I also have to get a tux. I'm sure the ball is formal."

"I wish you'd said something," Jenna commented. "We could have brought yours with us."

"I only got the invitation today."

"An English cut tuxedo from Saville Row would be very nice, dear," his mother said with a keen smile. "I don't suppose there'll be enough time to get one tailor-made."

"Off the rack will be fine, or I may have to rent one. This is hardly the time to be spending large sums of money on frivolous luxuries."

His father shook his head. "Don't fret about the money, son. We're not impoverished yet."

"That's encouraging. *Yet.*"

"I mean it," Thomas said. "We're going to get through this."

What would Devon say to such a supporting family?

Brent wondered. It was sad that she'd never had the experience, and a mark of her strength and character that she'd turned out to be so decent without one.

"Okay. Thanks. The second thing will be catching up on my protocol. Or rather learning it. I'm going to be rubbing elbows with the aristocracy this weekend. We don't run into too many dukes and counts and barons in Kentucky. An occasional honorary colonel is all, but I don't expect to find too many of them at Morningfield Manor, even fewer in white linen suits and string ties."

Jenna laughed. "You'll do fine, dear. Just remember to always say please and thank you."

"Yes, Mommy." They grinned at each other.

"This Camberg," Thomas said thoughtfully. "He sounds like a dangerous man."

"Be careful, dear," Jenna implored.

"Don't worry about me," he replied. "You just take care of my girls."

Thirteen

Wednesday, January 14

Brent had been to Morningfield Manor on his first visit
to England, when he'd flown over to confer with Nolan
Hunter and get as much information as he could about
Apollo's Ice. He'd first met Nolan at his flat in Mayfair,
and together they'd traveled by train to Cambridge, where
a chauffeur-driven car had been waiting for them at the
station. The visit had been brief. He'd arrived late one
afternoon and left early the following morning, all of it
in a dense fog that had him expecting to find Sherlock
Holmes in a deerstalker cap skulking around every
corner, magnifying glass in his hand. Unfortunately,
he hadn't run across the famous detective. He could
have used his help to solve the Case of the False Sire. He

hadn't seen very much of the exterior of the manor, either. The interior he recollected as being sedately comfortable, even luxurious in an old-fashioned way. None of which had mattered. His only interest at the time had been in the stables.

"Does Nolan know we're coming?" Brent asked.

Devon slowed her Austin as they reached the crest of a hill overlooking the sprawling estate. This view had been hidden in fog and rain clouds on Brent's first visit.

"Wow!" he exclaimed now as he leaned forward and peered through the windshield, or as Devon called it, the windscreen.

She smiled with obvious pleasure. "It is impressive, isn't it?"

They started down the sloping lane to the house. Peeking through the dense branches of leafless trees to the distant right, he glimpsed the black-slated roofs of what he imagined were the stables he'd been in last time, though he couldn't be sure. It was the fairyland castle in front of him that commanded his full attention.

"It's beautiful," he said.

"A bit of a hodgepodge," she admitted. One she obviously admired.

Brent had to admit there was something magical about it even in the winter with the trees bare. For her, he suspected it hadn't always been a fairyland of happiness, yet she could still see its beauty.

"Maybe," he replied, "but it all seems to fit together perfectly."

The complex of buildings was an eclectic mixture of architectural styles: Norman, Crusader, neoclassic, Georgian, Victorian. The central structure was of fitted gray granite, but several of the wings and extensions were in red and brown brick. There were towers and turrets, a cupola or two, mostly of black slate, but also a small section that was aged Spanish tile.

"Was it planned this way, or did it just happen?" he asked.

She laughed. "The oldest parts go back to the twelfth and thirteenth centuries, but there's not much of them left. Most of the pile was built in the early eighteenth century. The newest portions were added before the First World War, when a few nineteenth-century modifications were torn down because they were plain ugly."

"Well, the leftovers are just right."

She grinned over at him. "I'm glad you like it."

She pulled to a stop in the gravel courtyard and opened her door. Almost immediately a butler appeared and greeted her.

She introduced Giles to Brent. To the man's momentary surprise, Brent extended his hand.

"Welcome to Morningfield Manor, sir."

"Is my brother here?" Devon asked.

"Yes, milady. He's in the billiard room."

"Would you put Mr. Preston's things in the Ogden suite, please, Giles?"

"Yes, milady."

"Come on," Devon said to Brent. "Let's find Nolan."

Brent remembered the billiard room from his last visit, though he wasn't sure he could have found it again on his own. He and Devon's brother had played several games of pool on his one night in the manor, as they discussed the mystery of Leopold's Legacy's provenance.

They found Lord Kestler bent over a snooker table

with a pool stick in his hand. He had to have heard their approach, but he completed his shot, which was accurate, before straightening up to greet his guest.

"Good to see you again, old chap. I was amused when Mother told me you'd come to England, and fancy you just happened to drop by Devon's school." He passed off the innuendo with a jovial shrug. He was wearing a dark green woolen shirt with a darker silk ascot at the neck, the very image, Brent thought cynically, of an English nobleman relaxing in his ancestral digs. He put the stick to the side and extended his hand. "I do hope you're enjoying your visit. Delighted to hear you'll be joining us for the ball."

"Thank you for having me," Brent said, as he returned his host's firm grip. "Marcus told my mother your sister taught school. He didn't mention how beautiful she is."

Brent could feel the anger rippling off Nolan and the distinct discomfort on Devon's part.

"How…?" Nolan gave his sister a quick cautionary glance. "I'll explain later." She studied him with a glowering stare, and for a fraction of a second Brent thought he detected sadness in the viscount's eyes. It was so unexpected, so inappropriate, and the moment passed so quickly that he wondered if he had actually seen it at all.

"She is beautiful, isn't she?" Nolan remarked.

Devon started, clearly embarrassed at being talked about. "I thought I'd show Brent to his apartment—I put him in the Ogden suite—"

"Very convenient," Nolan said in a way that made Brent wonder if there was a hidden meaning in the remark. For a heartbeat he entertained the fantasy that his accommodations were connected with hers by a common door.

"Then I thought we'd have tea," she went on. "Care to join us?"

"I'm not hungry. Why don't you two run along? Take him on a tour of this old pile."

"Thank you again for having me," Brent said, offering his hand once more, as if the greatest honor had been bestowed on him by being allowed to stay here.

The gesture clearly caught his host off guard. "Not at all, old boy," he said, in a more spontaneously friendly manner. "Glad to be of service."

Devon led Brent back through the confusing labyrinth of corridors and chambers.

"I don't mean to be disrespectful," he said, "but may I ask what you do with all these rooms? I mean…what function do they serve? How many are there, anyway?"

She laughed. "Forty-six. And, you're quite right, most of them are useless. Like this one."

They were traversing a squarish room with an elaborately molded ceiling and heavy bronze chandelier, dark wallpaper and upholstered furniture that appeared big enough to swallow all but the largest people. Several portraits hung on the walls, as well as a few landscapes. In Brent's estimation, none of them were particularly interesting or even well-done—at least he couldn't imagine people actually looking like the ones depicted, but then he knew very little about art.

One of the tables, perhaps a yard square, had a checkerboard top of inlaid white and black marble. Brent felt reasonably certain a nearby cabinet contained one or more sets of chess pieces. It seemed an extravagant waste of space, however, to devote an entire room to an occasional game, especially a room, which in his estimation, was depressingly ugly.

"I'm sure the antiques are very valuable," he said diplomatically, as they moved on, "but…"

The next chamber in the chain was very different. Everything here was silvery and delicate, starkly light and feminine in comparison.

"I've been trying to convince my mother to unload most of this stuff and redecorate," Devon admitted, "but she's rather set in her ways, and since she rarely comes into this wing of the house she forgets how useless and uninviting it is."

"I assume Nolan will inherit the house at her passing."

"He says he'll sell it, when the time comes."

"You don't sound happy about that."

"This place is expensive to staff and maintain," she conceded, "and there are probably better uses for the house and land than as an occasional summer and holiday retreat for three people—"

"But it's home." He completed the thought for her.

They went through a small door to a narrow staircase that Brent suspected would at one time have been used exclusively by servants. He followed her down one flight to an expansive kitchen with a coffered ceiling. It smelled richly of baking bread, roasting meats and sweet spices. Brent's mouth watered.

A stout woman in a wraparound white apron rushed over to greet Devon with outstretched arms. The two women hugged.

"Augusta, this is Brent Preston. He's an American who will be staying with us through the ball."

"Pleased to meet you I'm sure, sir," she said, "and welcome to Morningfield Manor."

"Gussy, we're starved. I was hoping you might be able to prepare us a couple of sandwiches."

The woman's face lit up, as if Devon had said exactly the right thing.

"Indeed I can, miss. I have a joint of cold lamb and some nice fresh-baked bread, not an hour out of the oven."

"Thank you, Gussy, I knew you'd come through."

Devon led Brent to a raw-wood-topped table under a deeply cut high-arched window.

"Tell me all the gossip," Devon invited the cook, who was bustling around, giving orders to a nervous younger woman.

"Been quiet, it has, these last few weeks," Gussy prattled on, "what with His Lordship away so much. Except for all the preparations for the ball, of course."

"Do you have a copy of the guest list?" Devon asked.

"I do. Her Ladyship is very particular about making sure that everything we prepare suits. You know how we have to leave out onions in some dishes because Lady Winslow can't abide them, and how we always make sure there are those special capers to go with the smoked salmon for the marquis." The woman went to a battered wooden desk in a corner of the big room, picked up a clipped sheaf of curly-edged papers from the drawer and brought it over.

Devon skimmed each page, as if she weren't looking for anyone special, though Brent knew there was only one name on the list either of them was interested in.

"Lady Ilsa," Devon said. "I'm glad she can make it this year. She was ill last. Mr. Claxton. Lord Dexter-Ridley. We must make sure the orchestra play 'The White Cliffs of Dover' for him. Oh dear, Princess Gregoria. I do hope her English has improved. I don't think I understood more than six words the dear woman said to me last time, until I finally turned the conversation to French. Then we got along splendidly. The Duke of Camberg is coming, too."

"He's been here several times over the past couple of months, milady. Most recently two days ago," the head cook remarked, her tone not quite disguising her displeasure.

"Drinking heavily, I suppose," Devon muttered as she continued to peruse the list.

The other woman hesitated. "And getting your brother to drink too much, as well, if you'll pardon me saying. None of my business, of course."

The two women continued to chat about various aspects of the preparations under way for the ball and the people on the long guest list. Brent only half listened, since none of the names meant anything to him with the exception of Camberg.

As the younger servant set out dishes and serving utensils on the table, Brent realized he was famished. The smells of beef, pork and poultry roasting in the large commercial-size ovens only added to his appetite. Augusta prepared tea in a huge ceramic pot, while her young helper heaped a variety of side dishes and condiments on the raw wooden table: sliced tomatoes and purple onions, leaf lettuce, Greek olives and pickles, as well as pots of butter, mustard and horseradish. Finally the head cook produced a large, oblong loaf of coarse white bread, which she cut into thick slices with a serrated knife, and a leg of lamb from which she carved off generous portions of lean meat.

After tea, Devon continued to show him around the castle.

"There's an incredible amount of wasted space," Devon remarked, "and some parts of the building we've more or less permanently closed off. Getting permission to alter structures that are on the national register is time-consuming and requires a good deal of coordination. Mother, I'm afraid, isn't really up to it."

After half an hour of wandering through rooms and passages, they walked into a small courtyard, secluded among towers and battlements. It was in winter hibernation now, but Brent could easily imagine it exploding with colors, the classic English garden.

"This is your favorite spot, isn't it?" he asked, but it was more a statement than a question.

"How did you know?"

"Because the tension seemed to melt from your shoulders and your face softened the moment we stepped out here."

"I didn't know I was that transparent." She said it lightly, but there was a note of annoyance, as well, as if her privacy had been violated.

He wondered how many times she'd sought refuge here, away from whatever crises might be playing out within the walls of this storybook castle. Transparent, she said. He wanted to tell her she was transparent only to someone who was willing to take the time to see her as a whole person. He suspected the lords and ladies within these walls were too self-absorbed to see anyone else, even a damsel crying out for love and affection.

Indifferent to who might be looking out the windows above and behind them, he found her hand and encased it in his own. "It's peaceful and quiet. I can imagine you curled up there—" he pointed to a wooden bench between two towering yew trees "—reading Jane Austen or one of the Bronte sisters."

"Sometimes you scare me, Brent. Remind me never to underestimate you." A shy smile came to her lips. "I used to come out here when my father was in a mood. For some reason he never looked for me here."

"Or maybe he had just enough heart to grant you this sanctuary."

She stared at him strangely. "No one has ever suggested that, and I never thought of it myself," she admitted. "It's not very likely, but—" she rose up on tiptoes and kissed him softly on the cheek "—thank you for giving me the consolation of that possibility."

They left by a side gate behind two weathered Greek statues carved in granite—a couple of contemplative males whose power appeared both conscious and arrogant. A rust-colored brick path led them down a winding slope into a small wooded grove. As they emerged from it, Brent saw a massive stone-and-brick stable. Standing in the wide doorway was a man in his fifties, wearing baggy tan pants tucked into paddock boots, a thick woolen red shirt and black quilted vest.

Just the man Brent wanted to see.

Fourteen

They were fifty yards away when Devon said, "That's Brice Halpern, our head groom. He's been here at Morningfield Manor since before I was born, or Nolan, for that matter. He used to hide me away in the loft some times when my father was on a drunken tear. 'No, Your Lordship,' he would say. 'Haven't seen the young miss, but I'll tell her you're looking for her, if I do.' I've always felt safe around Halpern."

And yet, Brent thought, she calls him by his last name, like any other servant.

The groom smiled broadly at their approach.

"Mr. Preston," he said cheerfully, extending his hand before Devon had a chance to introduce him.

"Hello, Mr. Halpern. It's good to see you again. Have you been well? That hip still bothering you?"

On his earlier trip, Brent had noticed the groom's

slight limp but hadn't remarked on it until the man himself made a comment about not being able to ride His Lordship's favorite mount, Corsair, for several days, as promised, because his hip was acting up. Nolan had shown more displeasure than sympathy until Brice assured him he'd had one of the younger lads exercise the horse properly. Brent had inquired into the nature of Brice's discomfort and learned the groom had injured his hip some years before and was now having problems with arthritis in the joint.

The groom was clearly pleased that Brent remembered. "It's the winter bite, I reckon, sir. Spring'll bring it right."

"I see you two have already met," Devon said to Brent, clearly displeased at not having been told earlier.

"When I was here last time," he said, "Mr. Halpern was very helpful."

Clearly uncomfortable at being talked about, the head man turned to Devon. "Will Your Ladyship be wanting to go out riding today? I can have A Lady's Luck saddled and ready for you in a matter of minutes."

"A bit late today," Devon replied, then added, "but thank you. I thought perhaps in the morning."

"She'll be ready for you, milady, and glad to see you again. Welcome the exercise, too, she will. And for the gentleman I think perhaps Quillan."

She smiled. "Quillan. Yes. An excellent choice."

"Am I being set up here?" Brent asked with a suspicious grin.

"A spirited steed, Mr. Preston," Brice acknowledged, "but I vow nothing you can't handle."

"Just as long as Quillan knows that. How's Apollo's Ice doing?"

"Splendidly, sir. Would you like to see him?"

"Yes, I would. Thank you."

The groom was already turning into the shadow of the barn's interior. Without a thought for appearances, Brent reached out for Devon's hand but she maintained her distance as they followed the older man. At once they were enveloped by the humid warmth and unique smells of the equine world. Hay and grain, leather and liniment, and the animals themselves. He inhaled the sharp but not unpleasant aromas, smiling over at the woman a few feet away, but she was staring straight ahead.

She tightened her grip reassuringly, as if sensing how precious this realm was to him.

"Is Apollo's Ice standing at stud this year?" he asked the man limping ahead of them.

"No, sir." He detoured into a tack room. "His Lordship has decided not to have him cover any mares this season. Maybe after this terrible controversy is cleared up." He twisted a very large carrot from a bunch hanging on a peg next to a row of leather straps. They stepped outside again.

"I don't imagine there would be many takers under the circumstances," Devon observed.

"Quite right, milady. A pity it is, too, not just from your point of view, sir," he said to Brent. "He's a fine horse, Apollo's Ice. Did well on the track himself and has sired a passel of winners. A bit early for him to be retired. Still has several more years of productive work ahead, I should think. May I ask, Mr. Preston, if you've come any closer to resolving the matter?"

"Unfortunately not," Brent answered. "But I haven't given up."

They arrived at a stallion's stall, which was larger than

those allotted to mares and geldings and was heavily reinforced in case the animal became aroused and tried to
force its way out.

"Gentle, he is, sir," Brice pointed out, as he unlatched
the top grating of the iron gate and swung it out so they
could reach in and pet the horse.

As the three of them stood at the opening looking in,
its occupant eyed them from his crib where he was
munching on grain. He strolled over casually.

Devon extended her hand, fingertips held down, and
let the stallion sniff her. Brice snapped off a piece of
carrot and handed it to her. Displaying it on the palm of
her hand, she offered it to the horse. He sniffed it briefly
and took it unaggressively from her. Thirty seconds later
she was petting his nose.

"He is magnificent, isn't he?" Brent exclaimed.

Apollo's Ice was a medium to dark brown bay with a
black mane and tail and a well-defined clover-shaped
white star on his wide forehead. What made him instantly
recognizable from other bays with white stars even at a
distance, however, was a streak of flaxen hair that ran
through his long, full tail.

"Excellent conformation," Brent went on, "and beautiful gaits. The first time I saw the video of him I knew
he was a perfect match for one of our young mares,
Courtin' Cristy. And the offspring, Leopold's Legacy,
confirmed my judgment. He was on his way to winning
the Triple Crown, when this all blew up in our faces."

"It doesn't make any sense, sir," Brice commiserated.
"I keep telling myself there's some simple, logical explanation for what's happened."

"I intend to keep searching until I find it," Brent pledged. "Any word on Neal Caruthers?" He was the one groom Brent had been unable to talk to on his earlier trip to Morningfield. Caruthers had accompanied Apollo's Ice on his American trip four years ago, but had since moved on.

"No, sir. I've made some inquiries but no one seems to know what's become of him. Kept largely to himself, he did. Friendly enough chap but private, if you know what I mean. Didn't spend much time in the pub with the other blokes. Still, it's a small community. I reckon he'll turn up when he needs work."

When they returned to the barn door, Brent extended his hand. "I appreciate all your help, Mr. Halpern."

"My pleasure, sir."

Brent and Devon agreed to be at the stable at nine o'clock the following morning to go riding.

"You are full of surprises, aren't you?" Devon commented in a seething tone as they climbed the hill back to the manor. "You didn't tell me you knew Halpern."

"I told you I'd been here before," he replied, "and that I'd visited the stables to see Apollo's Ice. Of course Halpern was there. He's the head groom." He stopped at a little alcove in the path and faced her. "I never meant to deceive you, Devon," he said sincerely. "I hope you understand that."

She studied him, then lowered her eyes. "I guess I'm being paranoid."

He gathered her in his arms. "No, sweetheart. You're just being human. A lot has happened in the past few days, things that have turned your world upside down. We'll get things straightened out. You'll see."

He wondered at what cost, and at whose expense.

* * *

Dinner that evening was served at eight o'clock, a buffet set out on the elaborately carved sideboard in what the family called the dinette, a cozy eating room off the central hall overlooking the formal garden. Since the cook had said Charles had been a visitor only two days earlier, Devon wondered if he was still in the area and might make an appearance. Brent said he was eager to meet this nobleman whose standards of behavior, he claimed, were no better than those of a *Sopranos* thug. Devon had to admit she was eager to see how the two men would hit it off. When she inquired, however, Nolan's response was that there would be just the three of them that evening.

"You said nothing about coming to England when we parted in Kentucky only last week," Nolan commented to Brent in what sounded like a casual, friendly tone, but which Devon recognized as repressed anger. "Is this about Apollo's Ice? We've been over it so many times, Preston. I don't know what more I can tell you."

Her brother's use of their guest's last name when previously he'd been using his first was a clear indication of his displeasure. She looked at Brent to see if he appreciated the significance. If so, he was masterful at hiding it.

"It was a last-minute, sort of impulsive decision," Brent replied.

"How very interesting," Nolan mused with undisguised sarcasm. "I would never have credited you with being the impulsive type."

Rather than take umbrage at what amounted to being called a liar, Brent laughed. "But then we're not all we appear to be, are we?"

Nolan seemed unsure how to respond to the comment. "Why aren't you in school?" He nearly attacked his sister in compensation.

"You make me sound like a truant," Devon objected, trying to match Brent's lightheartedness. "I decided to take some time off to show Mr. Preston around and help Mother with ball preparations."

Nolan sneered. "Mother has things well in hand, as I'm sure you know. She's never needed your help in the past, and I doubt she'll welcome your interference now."

"Get up on the wrong side of the bed this morning, brother dear?" Devon chided with a forced smile. "That would have been some time ago. You should have got over it by now, or are you cranky because you didn't get your afternoon kip?"

Nolan's jaw tightened as he glared at Brent in a way that implied he was responsible for his sister's offensive attitude. Almost as quickly he made an attempt at a carefree smile. "You're going to give our guest the impression we do nothing but snipe and bicker, dear sister. Which, of course," he said to Brent, "is untrue."

Brent laughed without restraint. "You forget that I have a younger sister, too. Melanie and I might snarl and sputter at each other in private, but she knows I'd gouge the eyes out of any man who offended her. I'm sure you feel the same way about Devon."

The air thickened for the next ten seconds. Devon gazed at her brother and waited for his answer. He refused to meet her eyes.

The tension was lingering too long, and having made his point, Brent asked, "So what's the story with Quillan?"

"Quillan?" Nolan asked.

"My mount for tomorrow when Devon and I go riding together. I'm looking forward to checking out the rest of the estate, since the fog prevented me from seeing things clearly last time I was here."

There was a slight hesitation before Nolan said, "Ah. Quillan. Yes. A good choice. A ten-year-old Thoroughbred gelding. Smooth gaits, nicely spirited. We'd hoped he'd make a good steeplechaser, but he never quite measured up. Hasn't got the wind for the long haul. An enjoyable saddle horse, though. I believe you'll find him satisfactory."

"Is that why you gelded him?"

"No good for breeding," Nolan replied.

The rest of the meal passed in silence, broken only by the sound of sterling silverware tapping bone china. Finally, showing no more deference to his guest than common courtesy dictated, Nolan rose from the table, excused himself and left the room.

"Why were you trying to provoke him?" Devon challenged angrily.

"To see how he would react. To let him know I am no longer fooled by his nice-guy act."

"Wouldn't you get more help from him if you treated him as a friend and ally?"

"I've already tried that, Devon. He's not a friend. That's the point." He took her hand. "What do you want to bet that if he hasn't already done so, he's calling Charles at this very minute to let him know I'm here as your guest?"

She withdrew her hand and stood up, putting her back to him. "You're making him *my* enemy, too," she murmured, as tears began to choke her voice.

Brent rose and moved up behind her, placing his hands on her shoulders. She stiffened even more, willfully this time, hoping her taut posture would keep him from feeling her tremble.

"I'm not making him anything," he said. "If he is your enemy, and I hope he's not, it's by his own choice, his actions, his attitudes, not mine."

Gently, he brought her around to face him, though she kept her head bowed, her eyes averted.

"Don't you understand?" she cried, as she pressed herself to his chest and encircled his waist. "Nolan's the only family I have. You have your parents, your sister and brothers, your grandfather, and your children. I have no one except my brother."

"Your mother—"

She shook her head. "I've wanted to go to her for support and affection since I was a little girl, but I've not been able to. Pitiful, isn't it? My own mother. She was always too ill, forever going through one medical crisis or another. It's been her way of keeping us apart."

She pulled away, because touching him felt like a sign of weakness, and she was determined not to be weak ever again.

"My mother knew what my father was like, but she never tried to stand up to him for me, never really tried to protect me. Maybe she couldn't. I don't know. All she ever told me was that I had to be strong. I was a child, and she wanted me to stand up for myself against that brute."

"Did he hit you?"

"Sometimes. I learned quickly to stay out of his reach."

Brent shook his head, as if it were all incomprehensible to him. And maybe it was. His family experience was so different.

"The only one who ever tried to protect me was Nolan, and now you want to take him away from me, too."

"That's not true. If Nolan is the decent man you say he is, I couldn't drive him away with a team of horses. You know that as well as I do."

"Why is this happening?" she cried. "I don't understand what I've done."

"Maybe it's not what you've done, but what he's done."

She stared at him. "What do you mean?"

"I don't know. But if he really was the good guy you say he used to be, something happened to change him. Any idea what that could be?"

She admitted she didn't.

"Maybe when we get an answer to that question," he commented, "we'll have the answer to the others."

Brent had been hoping to spend time alone with Devon that evening, and Nolan's abrupt departure from the dinner table had encouraged that notion. But it was not to be. Because the manor had come down from the Morningfield side of the family, Lady Kestler had effectively made it an open house to her relatives—often, Brent learned, to the displeasure of Devon's father. This piece of intelligence tended to reinforce Jenna's speculation that the aging invalid was very much in control of the Kestler estate, rather than merely a beneficiary of it.

Within a few minutes of Nolan's leaving and before Devon and Brent had vacated the dinette, Perkins announced the arrival of Sir Baldric.

Devon's face immediately broke into a wide grin.

"Come on," Devon said, jumping from the table. "You'll like Baldy."

In the entry hall, surrounded by suitcases and trunks, a tall, lanky gentleman was pulling off kid driving gloves when he saw Devon. The gloves went flying in two different directions as he spread his arms and welcomed her into them.

"I'm so glad you're here," she cried out.

"Hortense is on the warpath, so I figured I'd better skedaddle. You must be the American," the florid-faced new arrival said, extending his hand to Brent. "Sarah told me you were here."

Devon made the formal introduction.

Dr. Sir Baldric Morningfield, Brent soon learned, was Sarah Morningfield's first cousin. Three years her senior and a confirmed bachelor, he had earned a life knighthood nearly twenty years before for his contributions to the discovery of DNA.

"Have you eaten?" Devon asked.

"Nothing scientifically credible, but yes. What I need is a drink. You will join me, I hope. I don't mind drinking alone, but I hate being the only audience for my utterly fascinating tales."

The luggage was quickly dispatched to his quarters, a suite of rooms permanently reserved for him in the same wing in which Sarah herself resided, and the three of them retired to the drawing room where the loquacious research biologist proceeded to regale them with stories of his travels.

Hortense, Brent was quietly informed, was Baldy's research assistant of twenty-plus years, and reputedly his mistress. She would be joining them the following evening. Tomorrow afternoon, Baldy, who took no offense at the nickname, hoped to be able to get in some shooting.

The evening was indeed very entertaining. The knight of the realm proved to have a formidable capacity for single-malt whisky. It was well past midnight when they retired to their separate rooms. So much for Brent's previous plans to spend the night with Devon.

Fifteen

Thursday, January 15

The low-angled winter sun was shining when they made their way after breakfast to the stable. As was his custom, Sir Baldric was sleeping late. Brice had their horses saddled and ready. Devon's horse, A Lady's Luck, was a well-groomed twenty-year-old dappled gray pleasure mare. Devon greeted the animal with soft words and gentle caresses. The glint in the horse's eyes and the way she responded to her mistress's touch made it clear she was happy to see her.

The gelding selected for Brent was a black, seventeen-hand warmblood, young and restless. Brent soothed him with a steady hand and calm words.

Brice gave Devon a leg up, while Brent mounted Quillan on his own.

Unfamiliar with the ground, Brent let Devon lead the way. The estate was extensive and they had a choice of several paths. They wound around fallow fields that would be planted in oats and barley come spring and into forests that were well maintained.

"It was one of the few things I was proud of my father for," Devon explained. "His conservancy. I wouldn't call him an environmentalist, but when it was suggested that certain stands of trees be cut and replanted, he adamantly refused. Mother, I think, was willing to let the old growth go, but Father was not. One would have expected their attitudes to be quite the reverse."

Brent had to agree. Of all the things he had heard and read about Nigel Hunter, his conservationism wasn't among them. Perhaps it should have been, to give a more balanced picture of the man.

Dark gray clouds began to skitter across the winter sky.

"Maybe we ought to head back," Brent remarked, as the first drops began to ripple through the bare trees.

"We'd be drenched by the time we got there," Devon responded. She brought her horse a quarter turn to the right. "Follow me."

She kicked her mare into an extended trot while keeping to the high crown of a rutted road that ran off at an angle from the path they had been following.

Brent trailed closely behind, enjoying the sight of her shapely derriere gracefully moving up and down as she posted ahead of him. On both sides of them, the bare limbs of the trees whipped in the wind like sharp claws beseeching the angry sky. A thatched cottage, like a vision from a nursery rhyme, came into view. On its far side was a sheltered area like a carport attached to the building. Devon ducked her head as she coaxed A Lady's Luck under it and slid lithely out of the saddle.

Brent dismounted before reaching the wooden lean-to and led Quillan under the cover. They tied the horses to a hitching rail suspended between two poles.

"Is it open? Do you have the key?" he asked, looking at the back door of the house.

"I brought it with me," she said with a smile. "Just in case."

"Smart girl."

She dug into her snug jodhpur pocket and extracted what looked like an old-fashioned skeleton key, which she used to open the heavy plank door. Once inside, however, she quickly crossed the room to a keypad and poked in a code.

He laughed, and she turned to look at him. "What's so funny?"

"How old is this house?"

"I don't know for sure. Two or three hundred years. Why?"

"With a hi-tech electronic security system."

She saw the irony and laughed, as well. "Actually, I don't know why we even bother. It used to be the estate forester's cottage, then my father used it as a stopping point for drinks on fox hunts, but we quit having them after he died. There's nothing of any great value here."

He looked around and, from what he could see, he had to agree. The wooden kitchen table and straight-back cane-bottom chairs were far from new, but he doubted they would qualify as antiques.

"Because it's yours," he said, "and that gives you the right to protect it."

She led him into the main sitting room, where a great stone fireplace dominated the far wall. On the left was the front door flanked by two small, not quite square casement windows. In front of the great hearth was a couch covered in a large floral pattern and two side chairs with similar slipcovers. Devon flipped a switch at the end of a pair of exposed wires running up the coarse plaster wall. A series of lamp sconces cast the room in a soft, golden glow.

The air was chill and damp and possessed a hint of the dankness of woodland earth.

"Are we going to be here long enough for me to light that fire?" Brent asked, noting that one had been laid, ready for a match.

Her eyes met his and the smile in them danced. "I hope so."

He did, too, and couldn't help but wonder if her objective hadn't been to bring them here from the beginning.

Long-taper matches stuck out of a crockery cylinder on the hearth next to a black iron poker. He took one, struck it on a stone and touched it to the paper crumbled beneath the twigs. Within a minute the kindling was aflame and licking the larger pieces piled on top.

Devon folded herself on the couch. When he stood up and turned toward her, she patted the cushion beside her. He needed no second invitation.

He threw his arm behind her shoulders and pulled her into his side. She cuddled up against him and placed her hand on his chest, sending electrical warmth through him and making him instantly aware of the hardness of his body in contrast to her softness.

The scent of rain in her hair tickled his nostrils. In what seemed like a natural action, he kissed the top of her head. She gazed up at him with an inviting smile and his lips came down to meet hers.

The storm outside was nothing compared with the torrent of feelings and emotions roiling through Devon now, lightning strikes of intensity, scary and bright, giving her glimpses of pleasure too long denied. She moved against his chest, transfixed by the firm compactness of sinewy muscle, of heat and his vibrating heartbeat.

His hand, sure, gentle, tender, fondled her breast, found her nipple, caressed and teased it and brought her breathing to a halt. His tongue toyed with hers, aggressive and persuasive.

"I want to make love to you, Devon," he murmured, when there was enough space between their lips for words to escape.

Her heart quaking, she kissed him hard. The fire glowed, but its heat was meager, unimportant. It was the conflagration inside her, the throbbing, pounding depth of it that arched her back and made her thrust against him.

His sure hands brushed against her sensitized flesh as they unbuttoned her blouse. He pulled its tail from her jodhpurs. She unsnapped the waistband, only then remembering she still had her boots on.

Suddenly they were both laughing.

He slid to the plank floor, knelt with his back to her, tucked her right foot between his knees and leaned forward. She planted her left foot on his narrow butt and pushed. The boot flew off and almost landed in the fire. He did the same with the other boot, rocked forward and let the second piece of footwear join the first in the corner beside the hearth. Then he scurried to a side chair, ready to yank off his own boots.

Grinning fiendishly, she got up, placed one bare foot on the cushion between his legs and started to tug.

"Be careful with those pretty little toes of yours," he cautioned.

She wriggled them and laughed erotically. "Trust me, sweetheart, I have a different kind of footsie in mind."

Once his boots were off, he put a large log on the fire, then turned and gazed at her on the sofa. In that moment, she understood what it meant to be seduced by a man's eyes.

He sat at her side, reached over and tried to patiently help her slip out of her already-open blouse, but neither of them was interested in patience. Or capable of it. Blouse and shirt. Jodhpurs and riding pants. What started slowly grew to frantic movements. Fingers and hands, mouths and tongues. Appetites and hunger. Physical desire and carnal lust. Neither could get enough of the other. The touch. The taste. The sight. The smell. They all conspired in a frenzy.

Then, just as suddenly, they both stopped and gazed into each other's eyes. This time when he touched her, it was with reverence and devotion. When his mouth savored hers it was with a slow-burning, all-consuming passion.

The rain outside pounded with a steady drumbeat, but they heard only the pounding of their hearts. Lightning strobed the charcoal sky outside. All they saw was the confirmation of desire in each other's eyes. They felt only the electrical sensation tripping along their flesh and in their bodies.

When at last he entered her, it was as nothing she had ever experienced before, and for a precious moment she feared she could never experience this ecstasy again. But that didn't matter. There was only now. There would only ever be now, this moment in time.

The fire in the fireplace had been reduced to ashes by the time they dressed. The sounds of lovemaking had drifted away with the wind and the rain, yet the storm between them was still raging, still unquenchable.

Devon set the security on the house and on her heart before she stepped outside. If they never came back, if he went away and never returned, the precious moments they'd spent here would always be hers.

A Lady's Luck whickered her greeting when the cinch on the saddle was tightened. She threw back her head, as if to endorse the pledge Devon had just made.

For the rest of the day, life took on a surreal quality for Brent.

The time spent in the forester's lodge had been magical. Being with Devon excited him, made him feel alive again as a man. But in the sweet afterglow of their lovemaking, he couldn't help chastise himself for the experience. He and Marti had been married ten years. He'd never been unfaithful to her, never wanted to be. She had been everything to him. Nor had any woman tempted him since her death—until Devon. Now he kept asking himself if, in making love with her, he was being unfaithful to Marti.

He was certainly not unfaithful to his memory of her. Marti had filled a special place in his world, his partner in body, mind and heart. She was the mother of his children. None of that would ever change. As vivid and happy as his reminiscences of her might be, however, Brent couldn't ignore the fact that Marti was gone from this life, and the place where she had been was a void of loneliness that left him incomplete.

Then he'd found Devon. She filled that void, made him feel whole again. She didn't replace Marti. She wasn't another Marti. She was Devon, a unique and wonderful person. The human heart, Brent now understood, wasn't restrictive. It didn't put limits on the capacity to love.

That new realization freed him. It meant he could go on without guilt, without regret. Marti had been a part of his life, one he would always cherish. Devon was a new chapter, yet to be written.

Baldy regaled them at lunch with tales of his adventures in places as diverse as the jungles of Africa and the inner cities of Chicago and Buenos Aires where he conducted research on the long-term effects of certain spores common in densely populated areas. Nolan showed up toward the end of the meal, morose and clearly struggling with the aftereffects of overindulgence the night before.

More guests arrived to take up early residence for the weekend ball and wanted to know everything they could learn from Brent about Kentucky and the state of American horse racing. If any of them knew about the ban on Quest Stables' Thoroughbreds, they were discreet enough not to ask or allude to it.

Following their late lunch, Brent called his parents to determine where they were and how the girls were getting on. If the sounds coming from the other end of the line were any indication, they were all having a very good time.

Still later Thursday afternoon, Lady Kestler arrived in

her Rolls-Royce followed by another car carrying her baggage. Brent stood apart to watch.

"She always liked playing queen," Baldy said, walking up to join him on the small balcony outside the first-floor library.

"It must be difficult for her," Brent noted, "being limited in mobility."

"She's quite expert at making the best of it," her cousin responded, seemingly indifferent to her plight. "She's had plenty of practice."

Brent was tempted to ask for elaboration—like how long she'd been chair-bound and the exact nature of her disability. Since Baldy was not a medical doctor, such an inquiry seemed prying, but Brent quickly realized he didn't need answers to those questions. Baldy had told him all he needed to know. Brent would pass on to his mother that she could take satisfaction in knowing her evaluation of the dowager Lady Kestler's situation was substantially correct.

The casual, relaxed atmosphere that had pervaded the house over the past two days changed with Lady Kestler's presence. The evening meal, which was still served at eight o'clock, reverted to the small dining room rather than the dinette, and it was a more formal sit-down affair instead of the laid-back buffet-style gathering. Brent got the distinct impression Lady Kestler was holding court and very much enjoying it. No wonder she'd continued the Archers' Ball.

Two things happened on Friday that affected Brent. The first was the viscountess's request that her daughter help supervise last-minute preparations for Saturday night's festivities. That kept Devon sufficiently tied up that she and Brent were not able to go on their afternoon ride and rendezvous in the woods. Whether that was by design, he wasn't sure. The second was Brent's telephone conversation with his father that afternoon.

"Have you spoken with Andrew yet?" Thomas asked.

"No, I thought I'd call you first, find out how the girls are doing, or rather how you're putting up with them."

"They're no trouble at all. Why should they be? You need to talk to your brother."

"About what?"

"A man's body was found in an expensive house in Savannah, Georgia, a few days ago, an apparent suicide, but when Andrew asked if it might have been murder, the authorities would say only that in the case of an unattended death, they consider every possibility."

"What else could they say, Dad? But wait a minute. Why are you even bringing this up? Who did they find?"

After a brief pause, Thomas Preston said, "Ross Ingliss."

Brent said nothing as he tried to assimilate the information and its implications.

When the computer glitch at the Jockey Association led to the DNA retesting of selected Thoroughbreds and Leopold's Legacy turned out not to be the offspring of Apollo's Ice, Brent had sought out and interviewed everyone who was even remotely involved in the process of breeding and registering the foal. Of the dozens of people on the list, only two people proved unavailable—Neal Caruthers, the English groom who had accompanied Apollo's Ice to America, and Ross Ingliss, the technician at the registry office who'd actually recorded the breeding data. Brent's investigation showed that Ingliss had been personally responsible for entering the original data on all the offspring of Apollo's Ice that had turned out to be "in error."

Ingliss had resigned shortly after the computer glitch was discovered but before the discrepancies were found, purportedly to go to Russia to marry a mail-order bride. That turned out to be a fabrication, however, and Brent had been able to track the techie to a number of places, including New York City and a high-priced condo in Florida. He'd also uncovered Ingliss's name on the passenger list of a flight to the Cayman Islands. Brent seriously doubted the man went there for their white sandy beaches. Yet every time he got close to the guy, the man disappeared. Brent became convinced Ross Ingliss was intimately involved in the fraud. The question was why. Brent hadn't been able to find a relationship between Ingliss and any member of the Preston family, their employees or business associates, and Brent had dug deep.

Now Ingliss was dead, preceded by a vet and a groom who had attended Apollo's Ice—or rather, the stallion purported to be Apollo's Ice.

One thing was certain. Ingliss had to have been murdered, too.

"Still there, son?"

"Just thinking, Dad."

Another pause.

"The police may be able to discover who did it," Thomas posited.

"Maybe." Brent wasn't convinced that was going to happen, or if they did, that it wouldn't simply lead to another dead end. Whoever was behind the fraud was covering his—or her—tracks very well.

Brent asked to speak to his daughters, but they were more interested in talking to Devon. They did agree to tell him all about the places they'd visited with Grandma and Grandpa, while he tracked her down. He found her in the immense banquet hall, overseeing the hanging of heraldic flags. He handed over the phone, then felt like an eavesdropper, standing around self-consciously while his girls obviously recounted to her all the things they had already told him. She asked questions he hadn't thought to ask, laughed and joked with them, and eventually ended the conversation with a big kiss for each of them. When she handed the phone back to him, they had already hung up.

"Sounds like they're having an enjoyable holiday," she said, then called out, "Thanks," as she was coaxed away by a servant with a question.

As she disappeared among stacks of boxes and decorations, the irony of the situation struck him. Here he was in a castle, getting ready to attend a fancy ball and wondering if one of the guests, maybe even the host, might be a killer.

Sixteen

Saturday, January 17

The ballroom sparkled, as much from the glitter of the jewelry worn by the women as from the thousands of polished crystal prisms twinkling from the three chandeliers. A full orchestra played what Brent thought of as elevator music from a dais set up at the far end of the enormous hall. Tables lined the outside wall of twenty-foot high Palladian windows. Across the shiny dance floor, in front of the opposing tapestry-covered wall, servants were perpetually replenishing a gargantuan buffet table, the center of which was dominated by a huge ice sculpture of an archer.

On a raised platform inside the double doors of the hall's main entrance, Lady Kestler sat in her wheelchair, wearing a lavender ankle-length silk-and-lace gown. A multistrand choker of pearls disguised the sagging wattles of her neck, while a diamond tiara crowned her head. Even to Brent's unpracticed eye, the jewelry must have represented tens of thousands of pounds. Sarah Hunter may have been born a commoner, but she carried herself, even with oxygen prongs in her nose, like royalty born to the purple.

To her mother's left and slightly behind her, Devon greeted arriving guests, wearing a full-length teal satin gown that clung to her curves in all the right places. It was cut just low enough to hint tantalizingly at her deep cleavage, above which a single, large aquamarine pendant was suspended on a slender gold chain. Brent was mesmerized by her beauty and grace and had the urge to run up and cover her from other men's prying eyes.

To her right stood her brother, Nolan, in some sort of fancy uniform with braids and epaulets. Whether it was military or purely ceremonial, Brent didn't know. He observed a good deal of hand-kissing by guests, not only of the older women but of Devon, and he found himself feeling an unaccustomed jealousy.

"She's lovely, isn't she?"

Brent turned to a slightly overweight woman in her mid-fifties wearing a low-cut vermilion gown that displayed an impressive bosom.

"I'm Rebecca Allingford." She extended her hand in a manner that said she was expecting a shake, not a kiss.

He took it politely. "Brent Preston."

"The American. Yes, I've heard of you."

"I guess I stand out in a crowd like this."

She laughed, a throaty rumble that suggested familiarity with whisky and cigarettes.

"In a crowd like this," she said, "everybody stands out. That's the point. Take off all the overpriced clothes and we're all rather plain and in some cases downright ugly."

"Present company excepted."

"I'm not fishing for compliments, Mr. Preston. I just enjoy talking to people, at least until I get to know them well enough not to like them."

"But isn't that when they become most interesting?"

She cocked her head, regarded him, then let out a guffaw, causing heads to momentarily turn. "A very astute observation. I like you."

A waiter in livery approached carrying a silver tray of various drinks. Brent passed up the short glasses of neat Scotch and opted for red wine.

"Not a whisky drinker?" she asked, taking a flute of champagne.

"I'm a Bourbon man."

"I prefer a good sour mash myself, and I do miss the generous use of ice." She chuckled at his surprised expression. "I'm originally from Nashville. Becky Brixby back there, till I met Clive. I think it was the name that attracted me initially. I'd never met anyone named Clive before."

Brent finally recognized the name. Sir Clive Allingford had been a regimental commander of troops in Afghanistan.

"Forgive me for not recognizing your name, Lady Allingford. My condolences on the loss of your husband."

"Thank you, but you and I don't have to worry about the lady business. Becky will do."

He decided he liked the woman. "How long did it take you to learn to speak *propa?*" he asked in what he recognized must be a terrible imitation of an English accent.

She chortled conspiratorially. "A few more of these—"

she held up her glass "—and I won't. I still slip up and use *gotten* instead of *got* once in a while."

"I'm still impressed."

She sipped her champagne. "I understand you're investigating a horse-racing scandal."

He raised an eyebrow.

"There are probably fewer secrets up here than below stairs," she said with some amusement. "I bet you could use the lowdown on a few of these people. I'm not a gossip as a general rule, but I grew up on a horse farm in Tennessee. Nothing as grand as Quest Stables, to be sure, but we loved our four-legged critters dearly. I heard about this problem some people are having with the supposed offspring of Apollo's Ice, as well as about Lord Rochester's stallion in Dubai getting poisoned. It rankles." She nodded to a passing waiter and exchanged her half-empty flute for a neat Scotch. "So if there's anything I can do to give you a leg up, so to speak, in your inquiries, I'm at your disposal."

Brent glanced over to where Devon stood beside her mother, enthusiastically performing her social duties. Nolan had stepped over to one of the drinks tables, though a servant would surely have brought him anything he asked for.

"Perhaps we can find a quiet spot somewhere to sit down," he suggested to Lady Allingford.

"Best proposition I've had all evening. Only one, as a matter of fact. Come on. I know just the place."

"What the blazes is he doing here?" Charles asked Nolan sotto voce, as he handed the liveried barman behind the table his empty glass.

"My mother invited him."

"You should have disinvited him."

"And what would I have said to my mother?"

"What the bloody hell do I care what you tell your mater? I want him gone."

"He's staying here at the house. It's only for another day or two at the most." Nolan took a gulp of his whisky. "Then he'll no doubt be going back to America."

"You don't seem to understand, Kestler. I want him gone tonight. Now."

Frustrated with the man's intransigence and feeling helpless in the face of it, Nolan simply walked away, conscious of the glare stabbing him in the back.

It gave him a certain satisfaction, too. Charles knew very well his mother wasn't fond of him, thanks to an impolitic comment she'd overheard him make privately several years ago about her common origins. If he made a scene here, Sarah Morningfield Hunter, Lady Kestler, wouldn't hesitate to have him removed and would happily use the occasion to permanently ban him from the premises. Common-born she might be, but she knew her aristocratic prerogatives and wouldn't shrink from exercising them.

How much longer the situation could go on was the big question in Nolan's mind. Initially he'd found that distracting the duke was a suitable substitute for appeasing him, but over time Camberg had become increasingly demanding, and Nolan didn't see an end in sight.

"There you are," Devon said, as Brent approached. Her mother's caregiver had taken over control of her wheelchair, freeing Devon to mingle with the crowd.

The orchestra had transitioned from background music

to more lively popular tunes, suitable for dancing, and had turned up the volume.

"Shall we dance?" Brent asked.

"He's watching us," she warned.

"Good." Brent took her hand and led her out onto the dance floor. "I understand seeing and being seen is the primary purpose of these little get-togethers."

He pulled her dramatically into his arms and wheeled her around.

It didn't take more than a few steps for her to be lost in the rhythm of the music or to realize Brent Preston was a very skillful dancer. She should have known he would be and found herself looking forward to a slow number and the closer physical contact it would bring.

"I met the most interesting woman a while ago," he said, his arm around her waist.

"More interesting than me?" she asked.

He looked down and grinned at her, his seductive, dark blue eyes twinkling. "In a different sort of way. Becky Allingford."

"Lady Allingford?"

"She is quite a lady, isn't she? Told me all sorts of fascinating things. Did you know, for instance, that Charles Robinett was arrested last year on suspicion of drugging a horse at Ascot?"

"Really? I never heard anything about it."

"Most people haven't. It was all kept very hush-hush." He pronounced it "veddy" hush-hush. "Becky thinks the record may have been expunged, as well."

Devon couldn't help but smile. "Becky, huh?"

"Seems they had a witness but he suddenly recanted," he continued, "then disappeared."

"Nolan… My brother…?"

"No hint he was in any way involved. Doesn't mean he wasn't, of course."

"You insist on thinking the worst of him, don't you?" she sniped, anger sweeping her in spite of the pleasant smile she managed to keep on her face.

"I don't want to argue with you, Devon," he whispered close to her ear. He had to be aware they were being watched from the sidelines. "I'm on your side. I want the truth, and I think you do, too. Let's not fight over what we don't know and concentrate on what we do."

He whirled her around.

"For example, I know I love the feel of you in my arms. I know I find myself intoxicated by the scent of your skin and the glow I see in your eyes when we make love."

Warmth rose to her cheeks, undoubtedly bringing color with it, for he broadened his grin at her.

As the musical selection transitioned to its final coda, he lowered his lips to hers and kissed her. She wanted—no, she needed—to resist him, but how could she when it felt so right, so perfect? Besides, she rationalized, she didn't want to make a scene. She could sense the eyes on her, feel the smiles turned in her direction.

She and Brent broke off, just as the music stopped. She was certain the applause that broke out was for them rather than for the musicians.

"Thirsty?" he asked, when the next number started.

"And nervous," she admitted. "I'm not sure that was wise, Brent."

"You didn't enjoy it?" he asked, feigning disappointment, and placed his hand possessively on the small of her back as he escorted her off to the side.

"Oh, I enjoyed it," she admitted. "Perhaps too much."

He chuckled. "There can never be too much joy, and I can never get enough of you."

"We're in a room full of people, Brent."

"I bet we can find one that isn't full." He leaned over and whispered in her ear, "Where it will be just you and me, and I can touch every part of you, savor the—"

She laughed. "You're incorrigible. This isn't the time or place, Brent."

"I won't argue with you about the place."

They continued toward the drinks table, greeting people along their way. Devon tugged his hand.

"He's there," she murmured.

"You'll be fine," he assured her, continuing to guide her, refusing to let her stop. "Champagne and a claret," he told the man behind the counter.

"Yes, sir."

"You're Preston," a deep male voice said from behind him. Devon felt her insides tighten, and for a moment she was afraid she was going to be sick.

Brent turned to him. "Yes, I am, but I don't believe we've met," he said in a pleasant enough manner. He didn't extend his hand, however, as would have been natural under the circumstances, but waited for the other man to initiate the courtesy.

"Charles Robinett."

"Ah, Camberg. Yes, I've heard of you." Brent had to know that for him to use the other man's titled name without the title was inappropriate to the point of being impolite.

Nolan came up on Brent's right. "How about a dance, sis."

Brent reached for her hand and squeezed it gently.

"Not right now," she said.

"I really think—"

"Thanks, Nolan," Devon said more conciliatorily. "Maybe later."

Her brother remained by her side, stiff shouldered.

The bartender moved a flute and a wineglass forward and backed off discreetly, aware undoubtedly of the tension sparking among the three men. He looked as if he would welcome the distraction of filling another order, but suddenly the people who had gathered around him seemed to have lost interest in renewing their drinks.

"You would do well to stay out of other people's affairs," Camberg said.

"Sage advice," Brent countered flippantly. "I've given it myself on occasion."

"Perhaps you haven't been informed. I've asked the lady to marry me."

"Two years ago, and she rejected you. Seems to me that terminated your…relationship."

"You're out of your league here, chap. We've merely had a lovers' spat. Nothing more."

"Oh, I don't think so." Brent smiled. "But I'll be very happy to discuss it further with you. Here and now or—" he winked at Devon "—at another time and place. At your convenience, of course."

Brent picked up the two delicate glasses with steady hands. "Shall we find a table, darlin'. I bet you're hungry as well as thirsty." They started to move off, then he paused long enough to turn to the two men. With a nonchalant nod, he said, "Till we meet again."

Seventeen

Devon was shaking as they sat at a table that had been vacated only a few seconds before. A waiter was still in the process of clearing dishes. Thank God Brent hadn't handed her the flute. Most of it would be either on the floor or on her gown.

She nodded distractedly to a passerby and sat mechanically in the chair the waiter had pulled out for her. Aware people were watching her, she kept the smile pasted on her face and looked up at Brent as he placed her drink in front of her.

"You did very well," he said, as he held up his glass to toast her.

"All I did was say no."

"It's not always an easy word to say."

"Why are you provoking him?" she demanded. "You practically challenged him to a duel."

"Do they still do that sort of thing in this country?"

"Stop joking, dammit. You're making matters worse."

He offered her a sympathetic smile. Its warmth helped, but it wasn't enough. She wanted his arms around her. She wanted the two of them to be somewhere else, notably the forester's cottage.

"Devon," Brent said as softly as the noisy room would allow, "you know I would never do anything that might hurt you. Never."

She reached for his hand. "I know, but—"

Trying to lighten the moment, he said, "I made my move. Now the ball's in his court."

She pulled her hand away.

"Devon, sweetheart, relax. I know what I'm doing. Please trust me. Yes, I goaded him into threatening me. In front of a large group of people. Now he has a choice. He can follow through, in which case he'll be breaking the law—"

"He's Charles Robinett, the Duke of Camberg. Don't you understand? He doesn't care about breaking the law."

"No, Devon, you don't understand. Do you remember when I told you I don't back down. Push me and I push back, except I push harder. Your aristocratic lord is a coward. He's also subject to the law. If he strikes me, I'll hold him accountable. If he doesn't, he'll lose face. Either way, I win."

She shook her head. "You really don't understand, do you?"

He put a finger under her chin and brought his lips closer to hers. "I understand I'm crazy in love with you." Then he kissed her.

Her eyes widened at his words—no one had ever said

them to her before—then his lips touched hers. Her heart leaped. The sensation lingered when he withdrew.

"Shall we dance?" he asked, as several people around them looked on and smiled.

It was nearly three o'clock in the morning when they finally left the ballroom and Brent escorted Devon back to her quarters. She invited him in but he declined. With the manor full of guests, there were too many prying eyes to afford privacy. Discretion seemed the wiser course under the circumstances, though he wanted desperately to make love to her.

"Sleep in," he said. "I'll wait for you in the dining room."

"If I'm not there by noon, you'd better come knock me up."

He grinned at her, tongue in cheek, barely able to contain the laughter bubbling up inside him. She played the sweet innocent for all of three seconds before she broke into a titter.

"Well," she said, "if you don't want to do that, will you at least kiss me good-night?"

But he already had her in his arms by the time she finished the sentence.

"I want a lot more than a kiss. You know that." His lips were a whisper away from hers.

They kissed. Hard.

"We'll go riding tomorrow," he said. "With any luck it'll rain and we'll have to find someplace warm and dry to wait it out."

"I'll pray for rain."

Despite the hour, Brent was walking on the balls of his feet as he made his way down the hall to his room. He'd closed the door behind him and was loosening his tie when there was a knock. His first thought was that Devon had followed him and was going to spend the night, or at least part of it, with him. But when he pulled the door open he found a member of the staff standing there.

"Begging your pardon, sir, but His Lordship would like to speak with you. He asked if you could meet him in the garden."

Brent's immediate reaction was to question why Nolan hadn't just come here, but of course he was the lord of the manor, in the literal sense. He didn't go to other people; they came to him. Actually, the garden sounded like a very good idea. He could use some fresh air.

"Please inform His Lordship that I'll be there in a few minutes."

"Very good, sir. Good night, sir."

Brent decided to change out of his monkey suit first. He replaced it quickly with casual slacks and the brown turtleneck his mother had insisted on buying him earlier in the week, then unlaced his oxfords and slipped his stockinged feet into loafers. He considered putting on his tweed jacket, as well, but in spite of it being the middle of January, the weather tonight was mild and there was no breeze, so the woolen pullover would be sufficient. He could easily guess what Nolan wanted to say and didn't expect it to take long.

He went down the back stairs that led directly to the basement. At their foot, to the right, were the kitchen, laundry and storage rooms. To the left, a frosted-glass-paneled door gave access up a short flight of outside steps to the back of the house.

He mounted the stairs, emerging behind a tall juniper into a small courtyard enclosed by a low stone wall. The formal gardens lay beyond. Starting across the brick path, he heard a rustling sound behind him. He barely had time to turn his head when he felt the first punch.

It grazed his jaw and sent him flying into a neighboring hedge. Instantly the attacker was on him, his fist upraised to deliver another punch, but the country boy from Kentucky was quicker.

Thrown back, he was too unbalanced to counter the jab, but he was able to shift his weight enough that the next fist slammed into the bush instead of his face.

The momentum of the swing destabilized his assailant. He toppled forward into the dry shrubs. While he tried to regain his balance, Brent caught a glimpse of what looked like a small red-and-gold tattoo on the man's flailing right hand. Brent rolled over and scrambled to his feet.

An old-fashioned fistfight ensued. A bare-knuckle brawl. At six two, Brent was more than two inches taller than his adversary, but the other guy had a good thirty-pound advantage, or rather disadvantage, because he wasn't nearly as agile as Brent.

Then a second assailant popped out of nowhere.

Brent didn't recognize them, except to know neither was Nolan Hunter or Charles Robinett, a fact he found rather disappointing. He would have loved to smash his fist into the face of either, but of course, cowards used proxies. How foolish he'd been not to consider the possibility of hired thugs. Devon had said her two dates had been attacked after taking her home and the culprits had never been identified. Surely they would have recognized Charles or Nolan, unless the two victims had been too intimidated to admit it.

Two against one. So much for the Marquis of Queensbury rules. But the odds were about right, Brent figured.

It had been some years since he had used his kick-boxing expertise, but some skills, like riding a bicycle or a horse, simply snapped back when the circumstances demanded. Even as his right foot came up and made contact with one opponent's elbow, Brent knew his muscles would be protesting bitterly tomorrow. But tomorrow was another day.

A knuckle connected with his right eye socket at about the same time one of his fists landed squarely on the nose of the other stranger. The cracking sound was unmistakable. The man went down.

Brent whipped around and connected a toe to the standing man's solar plexus and the guy went careening against, then over, the hedge.

"Go," the first man exhorted his companion, his voice muffled by the hand trying to stanch the flow of blood streaming from his broken nose.

In a matter of seconds, the two men were running in different directions. Brent considered pursuit, but they were more familiar with the area and had greater incentive for speed. It would have been nice to produce one of them for the police, but he doubted either would give up the name of the person who hired them.

Brent knew who was responsible, and so would everyone else when he appeared at breakfast in the morning with a black eye. He couldn't help but laugh. Camberg, the cowardly fool, should have waited another day, when nobody would be around.

Yep, he'd be sore as hell tomorrow and would no doubt look like hell, as well, but that wasn't important. He took consolation in knowing he'd stirred up a hornet's nest. No question now who the enemy was. Targets were much easier to hit when you could identify them.

As he doctored his face in the bathroom of his suite, he considered what had just transpired. Was it related to his investigation of Apollo's Ice? Men had been killed to keep that scam secret, yet he had received no more than a mugging by thugs. Incompetent ones at that. Of course, a murder at Morningfield Manor would be a scandal of major proportions and bring in authorities the Right Honourable Nolan Hunter, the Viscount Kestler, would definitely not welcome—a good reason for limiting the attack. Or was the ambush no more than the revenge of a jealous, spurned lover against his competition? The latter seemed more likely.

That he had gotten the better of his opponents in the garden was a source of some satisfaction, but then Brent thought of something else. The servant who came to his room had said "His Lordship" wanted to see him. As Brent recalled from reading about the English peerage, a duke would have been referred to as "His Grace." That meant that it had been Nolan who had summoned him to the garden, rather than Charles. Or had the two simply colluded in the attack? Either way, it also meant he now had two enemies to contend with.

Later, lying sleepless in bed, Brent remembered that one of his assailants had sported a red-and-gold tattoo on his wrist. He sat up straight. Hadn't his sister Melanie's attacker at Gulfstream Park had a similar tattoo? Maybe this attack had nothing to do with the duke and his jealously. Maybe Nolan had simply used the situation to warn Brent off.

Brent lay down with a groan. "Nice try," he muttered. "Either way, it won't work."

Eighteen

"My God," Devon exclaimed, when she sat down across from Brent in the breakfast room the following morning. Her plate clattered to the table and a banger rolled off onto the starched white tablecloth. She ignored it and shot around the corner of the table to examine his face. "What in the world happened to you?"

He smiled at her, though doing so smarted. "A late-night visitor, or I guess I should say early-morning visitors, plural, since there were two of them, but you should see the shape they're in."

"You joke about this?" She was aghast.

He gently removed her hand from his cheek and held it. "What would you like me to do, Devon? Believe me, this isn't as bad as it looks. In school I often came out worse."

"I don't understand men. They beat each other up, then laugh about it."

He was tempted by a retort about the mystery of women but decided this was the perfect time to observe the adage that silence was golden.

"Was it Charles?" she asked. "Did he do this?"

"Not personally. Please don't be upset, sweetheart. I know I look pretty bad, but it's only a black eye. No real harm done."

"But there could have been."

"Devon, honey, a lot of things could have been. Let's concentrate on what is. One of those things is that I love you."

He'd spent a good part of his wakeful night nursing his throbbing face and thinking about Devon, about them. He'd crossed a line when he'd told her he loved her. He'd said those words to only one other woman. For him they weren't just a statement. They were a commitment.

Instead of Devon softening as he'd expected her to, she grew very still. She wasn't used to being loved, he realized, or being told she was, and she hadn't yet said those magical words to him. But he could be patient.

She also wasn't placated. She must have realized arguing wouldn't do any good or make him look any better.

"So what now?" She resumed her seat across from him and put the sausage back on the plate with her fingers, just as a servant came over and poured coffee and hot milk into her cup. Brent declined a refill for the moment.

"Well," he replied seductively, "I was thinking about that ride we were planning to take."

"You want to go riding in your condition?"

"You make me sound pregnant." He chuckled at her shocked expression. "Think of it as therapy, good exercise for sore muscles."

"You're a glutton for punishment."

"I'm a glutton for you."

"You're sure you want to do this?"

"The forecast is for rain."

This time she did laugh and shook her head. "You're incredible."

"I do my best," he said, grinning. To hell with the pain. Seeing the gleam in her chocolate-brown eyes made it all worthwhile.

Baldy entered the morning room, looked around, saw them and came over.

"Good morning—" He stopped when he saw the condition of Brent's face. "Oh, I see you had your conference with His Grace. I trust he looks even worse."

"He sent thugs," Devon said, still outraged. "Two of them."

"Pity," the elderly gentleman commiserated. "Still, you're here showing your battered face and he isn't, so I'd say you won." He extended his hand. "It's been a pleasure meeting you, Mr. Preston. I hope we shall have an opportunity to meet again. Now I must be off." He gave Devon a hug. "Take good care of him, my dear. He seems a man worth holding on to."

Sir Baldric turned and left.

Brent and Devon ate a breakfast that was twice as big as any he usually ate at home. Thick rashers of bacon, scrambled eggs, kippered herring, grilled tomatoes, hearty slices of toast with butter and marmalade and two large cups of very strong coffee with scalded milk. He rationalized his appetite by calling it brunch which, considering the late-morning hour, it was.

"You're really hurt," Devon said, when he winced with stiffness getting up from the chair and came around to hold her.

"Nah, just flexed some muscles last night I haven't used lately. Moving around helps."

The soreness had, in fact, subsided by the time they reached the stable.

"Looks like you walked into a door," Brice Halpern remarked, when he saw Brent.

"You ought to see the door."

"I heard about your troubles during the night."

"Do you know who did it, Halpern?" Devon asked.

"Can't say I've heard anything, milady, but I'll let you know straightaway if I do. Now, I'll have your horses saddled and ready to go in a few minutes."

He motioned to a lad who'd been standing anxiously off to the side. "Chester, get A Lady's Luck ready for Her Ladyship."

"Right you are, guv. All brushed, she is, just waiting for the tack and saddle." He started into the stone barn.

"Would you mind going with him, milady," Halpern asked, "and show him which saddle you prefer?"

It seemed to Brent an odd request, but Devon took it in stride and accompanied the young man.

Halpern snapped his fingers to another lad and ordered him to bring Quillan up. When the second lad disappeared, it was just the two of them. "I was hoping I might have a word with you privatelike, sir, if you don't mind."

"Of course, Mr. Halpern. Has something happened?"

"Received word from a chap I know early this morning

that they've found Neal Caruthers." Caruthers was the groom who had accompanied Apollo's Ice to the States.

"That's good news," Brent said, then looked more closely at the older man. "Isn't it?"

"He was in a car crash, sir. In Scotland. No idea what he might have been doing up there. His family's from Cornwall, as I recollect. Holiday maybe, or he could have got a job there, I suppose."

"A car crash."

"Dead, sir. I'm sorry."

So was Brent. Caruthers had been his last hope of finding out firsthand who might be behind the breeding fraud. It seemed strangely convenient that the two people in a position to know—Ross Ingliss and now Neal Caruthers, both men under forty—had suddenly died within a short time of each other.

"Any evidence of foul play?" he asked.

"Can't say, sir. The chap who called me—I won't say Kev and me are close friends, just acquaintances from being in the same trade—heard about it from a colleague up north. Apparently it was in the Glaswegian *Guardian*. A local road incident, so it didn't get posted anywhere else, but Kev remembered Neal used to work for me, and thought I would want to know. Ran off the road late at night, the newspaper said. Hinted he might have been drinking. Could be. Neal was a good man, but he did like a nip now and then when he wasn't working. I never tolerate a drinker on the job, Mr. Preston. The lads all know that."

Brent believed him.

"Well, sir," Halpern continued, "I was telling Crispin, one of the older lads who used to be pals with Neal, about his death, and we got talking about how good Neal was with Apollo's Ice, and how Crispin was surprised when Neal decided to leave—"

"Left voluntarily? Wasn't fired or laid off?"

"Said he needed a change. I thought it odd at the time, but there's lads like that. Stay in one place very long and they get the wanderlust, if you know what I mean."

Brent nodded. It wasn't uncommon for people who worked with horses, single men especially, to move around.

"Anyway, we got talking about Apollo's Ice and this other lad, Danny Bridges, pipes up about something that happened about a month ago. His Lordship sold off a number of horses some time back. Routine transactions. Nothing unusual in any of them. Got fair prices, too. Well, most of them the buyers sent along their own horse boxes to transport them back to their new homes, but there was one or two we arranged the shipping for."

Brent nodded.

"Sent our own lads with those horses, I did. Didn't want to take no chances on them not getting to their destinations safe and sound."

"Very wise."

"Now Danny Bridges, he's one of the younger lads, but a good one, cares about the animals, he does, babies them a bit but all to the good. Well…Bridges tells me only this morning when we was talking about Neal and Apollo's Ice that he'd seen a horse in a pasture in South Dorset that could have been the twin of Apollo's Ice. Go on, I says, disbelieving. 'S truth, he swears. Even inquired in the neighborhood, he says. Name's Texas Tea, one of the local lads tells him. Been there only about a month, he claims.

'Course, that was over a month ago now. Can't say if it's still there, or even if Bridges's eyes might have been playing tricks on him. Would be unusual, though, him not getting it right, I mean. He knows horses, and Apollo's Ice is what you might call distinctive. Mind you, I told him to keep his yap shut. Wouldn't want rumors like that getting around now, would we? Probably just a mix-up."

A groom leading Quillan came into the light from the depths of the barn. Brice took the lead and dismissed the young man.

"Don't know if that helps, sir," he told Brent, as he pulled down the stirrups which had been set high in their straps until they were needed. "Just thought you'd like to know, maybe check it out for yourself."

"You're right. I will. Can you tell me exactly where this horse is located?"

"Lynch Farm, it's called. I took the liberty of writing it down." Brice dug into his shirt pocket and removed a slip of paper. "Village of Dinston Heath. Too small to be on most maps, not more than a few houses, I'm told. But you follow them directions I wrote down and you'll find it right enough. Bit late today for sightseeing, what with the rain coming and all," he added. "But if you set out early in the morning you shouldn't have no trouble."

"Thanks, Mr. Halpern. I appreciate your doing this."

"Watch out for doors, sir," he said with a grin, as Devon came into the light, leading A Lady's Luck.

Nineteen

They were in the Austin heading south, Devon at the wheel, Brent in the passenger seat on her left, his head thrown back, eyes closed.

"Why do you want to go to Dorset?" she asked.

He'd proposed this trip over breakfast in the morning room. Like Sir Baldric, most of her mother's relatives and the guests staying at Morningfield had departed the day before. So had Nolan. He hadn't stopped by to tell Devon he was leaving or even left a message on her cell phone. The schism between them seemed complete.

"To see a horse," Brent answered. "How long do you think it'll take us to get there?"

"I had a difficult time even finding the village you

mentioned on a map. Dinston Heath is hardly a thriving metropolis."

"I like small towns." He kept his head back and his eyes closed. "They're friendly. How long?"

"About six hours, depending on traffic. How did you even hear about this place, anyway?"

"Devon, how am I going to catch up on my much-needed sleep if you keep asking questions?" Brent complained.

With Nolan gone and her mother secluded in another wing of the sprawling pile, she'd invited Brent to spend the night with her in her room, which he had. Even now, the thought of them frolicking on that big canopy bed sent warm cascades racing through her. They hadn't slept much, but the memory of waking up with him molded to her.... She sighed. At least they'd been discreet enough to come down to breakfast separately, though within minutes of each other.

"I ought to make you drive," she said.

"That would be dangerous, sweetheart. As Katie would say, you know how to drive on the wrong side of the road. I don't."

"It's not the wrong side. At least not from my perspective."

He cracked an eye open and glanced over her way, that sexy grin of his curling his lips. "You know, I thoroughly enjoyed your perspective last night."

"Shut up and go back to sleep," she said with annoyance, but she couldn't keep from smiling all the same. It had been the most satisfying night she'd ever experienced, and she definitely wanted more.

"I can't. You keep talking."

She hit the brakes and swerved over to the narrow verge on the left.

"Okay, okay." Brent held up his hands in surrender. "Truce."

"Just remember who's in the driver's seat."

His eyes narrowed and twinkled as he gazed over at her. "Yes, ma'am." After a moment, he added, "Have I told you how much I like the way you drive? Last night—"

"Be quiet and let me concentrate." Which was getting increasingly difficult to do with constant reminders of the night they'd spent together.

A mile or two down the road, she said, "This horse…"

He sat up in the seat. "May be a ringer for Apollo's Ice."

She considered the information for a minute. "Who owns it?"

"I don't know. Only that it was being kept at a place called Lynch Farm. I don't even know if it's a stallion or a mare or a gelding."

"You said *was,* not *is* being kept."

"The information I received is about two months old," he admitted.

"Who told you about it?"

"That's not important, and I have no idea how reliable the information is. I'm getting it second- or thirdhand that a horse was seen in a pasture at this place that could have passed for Apollo's Ice. Except Apollo's Ice hasn't left your brother's stable."

Brent often accused her of not answering questions, at least not directly, but she didn't miss the fact that he wasn't answering hers now, either. Like who had given him this information? She wondered why he was holding back. To protect the source, obviously, but why did he feel he had to protect the source from her?

"And this person, whoever it is, chose to tell you about it, not the authorities?" she pressed.

"No reason to tell the authorities. They're not looking for Apollo's Ice or a horse that looks like him. I am."

"You seem to have made a lot of friends in the local area very quickly."

"It's us commoners, we have a secret handshake."

Was the remark intended as an insult? Clearly he wasn't in awe of titles of nobility, but then, neither was she. He, from his culture. She, from experience.

She said nothing, because she also knew the truth of his statement. Not the handshake part, but the attitude of *us* against *them.* She'd broken that barrier with Sybil and Heather back at the academy, but she'd never been able to break through in the same way at Morningfield. Except maybe with the cook. But even Gussy called her milady, or at least miss, never Devon. At first she thought it was because of her father, and while he was alive it probably was. He would have become incensed at her being familiar with the staff, and he would have fired any member of the staff who dared show familiarity toward her. But even after he died, the staff didn't completely lower their guard. It took her a long time to realize it was because of her mother—the commoner who had learned to put on airs,

"So what happens if we find this ringer?" she asked.

"We find out who owns it, where it's been. Standard investigative work."

"Elementary, of course." She held up her chin and said haughtily, "You may call me Watson."

"Oh, I can think of other things I would like to call you, darlin'."

She slid a glance over at him. "You do have a way with words, Sherlock."

"As for elementary, yes, I'd like to go back there, too."

"Not now. I'm driving."

He chuckled. "That does sound better than having a headache."

They stopped three hours later at a pub on the outskirts of Wareham, in sight of the ruins of Corfe Castle, to get a bite of lunch and ask for directions to Dinston Heath.

The publican was a friendly fellow with a rosy face and a barrel belly swathed in a white apron. He confirmed they were on the proper road.

"Would you, by any chance, know of a farm there run by Mr. Lynch?" Brent asked.

"Good man, John. Irish. From Belfast. Knows his ponies right well. Him and Mavis bought the place about thirty years ago."

After a Cornish pasty, a small salad and a half pint of bitter each, they were once again on the road. The publican's directions were spot-on. Twenty minutes later they pulled into a nearly invisible lane between fenced-off pastures.

"Stop," Brent shouted.

Devon hadn't been going more than ten miles an hour on the narrow, unpaved road. Nevertheless, she hit the brakes so hard they both lurched forward against their seat belts. Even before she had a chance to ask what he saw, Brent had his door open and was climbing out.

"What—"

"Come look." He pointed cross the winter-brown field. She stared, wide-eyed. "It…looks like—"

A satisfied grin lit up his face. "Apollo's Ice."

"You're right." She couldn't believe what she was seeing. "He is a dead ringer."

They stared for at least five minutes.

"Let's go talk with Mr. Lynch," Brent finally said.

Invigorated and curious, they climbed back into the Austin. Devon put the car in gear and proceeded toward a thatch-roofed cottage surrounded by yew trees. On the way, Brent told her about the approach he planned to use and asked her advice. They discussed it for only the few minutes it took them to reach the quaint house.

A woman of perhaps sixty-five in a housedress and bib apron came out to greet them as they alighted from the vehicle.

"Mrs. Lynch? My name is Brent Preston. I'm an American from Kentucky and I'm doing research on Thoroughbred horses. I was told you have some prime stock here, and from what I've seen in your field, the information is correct. Oh, excuse me. This is my English assistant, Devon Hunter."

The woman extended her hand. "Mavis Lynch. Yes, we raise Thoroughbreds. Come out to the barn. John is there tending to a colicky mare."

The Tudor-style horse barn behind the house, though possibly as old as the house itself, had a shingle rather than a thatch roof. A central aisle of timeworn brick separated ten stalls, five on each side, as well as a tack room and office area.

John Lynch, only an inch or two taller than his wife, was about seventy. He had a full head of white hair, an outdoorsman's ruddy complexion and brilliant blue eyes. He smiled easily in greeting as Mavis introduced their visitors.

In addition to the sick mare, there were three other horses in stalls, a gelding and two mares.

"I saw a stallion in your pasture," Brent remarked. "Nice head. Broad chest. Sixteen hands?"

"Sixteen two," John corrected. "Got him about two months ago." He spoke with a mild but unmistakable Irish brogue. "Seller claimed he was weak in the right fore, but to be honest, sir, I haven't found any evidence of it."

"You ride?" Devon asked.

"Not as much as I used to, but my grandson does. Exercises them all on a regular schedule. Wanted to be a jockey, but he grew too much."

"Taller than you are, Mr. Preston," Mavis said proudly. "By a good inch, I'd say."

"Expert rider, though," her husband added. "Born for the saddle."

"What's the stallion's name?" Brent asked.

"Called Texas Tea."

"Is he standing at stud?"

"Oh, I wish he were, Mr. Preston. Could get a pretty penny for him. But he's not registered."

"Pity," Brent agreed. "He sure has the lines of a Thoroughbred. One of the things we're trying to establish by our research is whether DNA can identify breed. As you know, that's not possible at present. We can verify the dam and sire of a given foal through DNA testing, but not the breed."

The horse owner nodded.

"Would you be willing to furnish a blood sample from Texas Tea? I'll pay for it, of course, and for the inconvenience to you. We would want it drawn by a licensed veterinarian. Yours, if he's available. I'll also need affidavits signed by him and you certifying the sample that we send to the Jockey Association."

Mavis looked at her husband. "Simon may be available today. Shall I ring him up?"

Twenty

Two hours later it had all been accomplished. Lynch's vet, Dr. Simon Davis, had drawn two blood samples. Properly labeled and packaged, one was sent by express courier to an equine lab in London, the other by FedEx International Priority to the Jockey Association in America. A detailed statement had also been taken by Devon from Mr. Lynch, explaining how he came into possession of the intact stallion called Texas Tea from a woman by the name of Muriel Fairbrown, who told him she had bought it from a man called Nolan Kestler. In none of the transfers were papers of pedigree attached to the bills of sale, establishing the colt or either of its parents as registered Thoroughbreds. That left the horse, who had all the recognizable characteristics of the breed, unregistered and unregisterable.

By the time they were ready to leave, it was dark and

a heavy rainstorm was predicted that would make a long nighttime drive back to Cambridge unpleasant. Mavis Lynch recommended an inn in Wareham with a view of the lighted thousand-year-old castle where they might spend the night.

The steep-roofed Tudor inn was every bit as charming and quaint as the horse owner's wife had suggested. By six o'clock they'd procured a comfortable, low-ceilinged room with an immense quilt-topped bed.

"I understand bits and pieces of what has transpired," Devon told Brent as they sat in the public room sipping the local bitter, "but can you put it all in context for me?"

He'd debated with himself last night and again today about whether he should tell her of his conversation with Brice Halpern. There were several reasons for not doing so.

One was Nolan. As much as she might be angry and disappointed with him, he was still her brother. Knowing how close Brent was getting to breaking the case, she might be tempted to warn him. If Nolan was willing to go along with Charles in attacking Brent for dancing with Devon, what level of violence might he be capable of?

Then there was Halpern. If Brent had told Devon last night about the new evidence he'd received, it would have been obvious that the head groom was the source. It might still be, but at least geographical distance delayed any face-to-face confrontation with the man who had protected Devon in the past.

Not telling Devon also protected her, Brent told himself. If this ended the way he thought it might, she would be able to honestly say she didn't know the source or depth of Brent's knowledge and was therefore operating in the blind. At some point in her relationship with her brother, whom she obviously cared for very much in spite of everything, that innocence might be crucial in mending the breach between them.

All well and good, but it bothered Brent that those explanations for his keeping secrets from her stemmed from one underlying assumption—that he couldn't trust her.

Was that true? He didn't think so. They'd known each other a very short time, but he'd also fallen in love with her. Or was it the pleasure he'd found in her body after years of sexual starvation that was clouding his mind?

And what would her reaction be when eventually she realized what he had done?

She'd played her part as a professional research assistant extraordinarily well, never giving a hint that she had a personal stake in the outcome of their findings. Even when the name Nolan Kestler had been mentioned she hadn't flinched, though the discovery meant disaster for her brother and the family name. If Brent really didn't trust her, he shouldn't have allowed her access to the evidence, but he had.

"There are some details I'm not clear on yet," he said, "so I don't want to speculate. It'll be better for you if I don't at this point, since it'll protect you later from accusations of having a prejudiced view."

She nodded, though he wasn't sure she completely bought it.

"The papers Mr. Lynch furnished us today," he went on, "show Nolan Kestler bought Texas Tea from Charles Robinett four and a half years ago. I know from talking with Brice Halpern back at Morningfield, shortly after Apollo's Ice sired Picture of Perfection here in England, he had three systemic infections in a row, accompanied by high fevers. The horse obviously recovered from each one, since he was sent to the U.S. to fulfill his breeding contracts there, but my guess is that in the process he was rendered sterile."

Devon understood the relationship between high fevers and sterility.

"But he was bringing in enormous stud fees," Brent went on. "Declaring him sterile would be like turning off a fast-flowing money tap."

"And Charles just happened to have an unregistered Thoroughbred that had the same markings as Apollo's Ice."

"Exactly. Whether the two horses are related is an interesting question I'd like to get an answer to, but that can wait. All that's needed at the moment is knowledge of the ringer's existence, and we've got it."

Among the other things they'd done was to take pictures of Texas Tea.

"It still doesn't make sense to me," Devon said. "Why not just substitute Texas Tea for Apollo's Ice?"

"I'm coming to that," Brent said. "Substituting one horse for another is trickier than it sounds. The grooms would be able to distinguish one horse from another, regardless of how much alike they might look to the casual observer. Even if your brother replaced all his barn staff—something that would undoubtedly raise all sorts of questions and suspicions—there would still be a fair chance that someone else would recognize the discrepancy. As we discussed the other day, horse lovers can distinguish horses as easily as I—and apparently your headmistress —can tell the twins apart."

"So how was it done?"

"Artificial insemination," Brent declared. "I even

know by whom. When Apollo's Ice was sent out to stand at stud, a groom by the name of Neal Caruthers always went with him. I think he took frozen semen from Texas Tea with him. After sterile Apollo's Ice covered the mare, Caruthers would artificially inseminate her with Texas Tea's fertile semen. The offspring would look sufficiently like Apollo's Ice that no one would question who sired it."

"But what about the registration process?" Devon asked. "The foal still had to be registered shortly after its birth, and that involves comparing its DNA with the DNA on file for the dam and the sire. Why wasn't the discrepancy picked up then?"

"Charles, or maybe your brother, had someone working at the Jockey Association registration office who could falsify the records. His name was Ross Ingliss, a technician who disappeared a few months ago. Unfortunately he died—maybe suicide, but I suspect murder—before anyone could get to him."

Devon took in a deep, disheartened breath.

"If there hadn't been a computer glitch," Brent went on, "if the DNA samples of certain stallions hadn't had to be verified, the chances of this substitution ever coming to light were very slight. Your brother would have continued to collect his stud fees, and mare owners would have gotten look-alike foals that would have been credited to Apollo's Ice without question. Clearly Texas Tea turns out competition-quality offspring. After all, our Leopold's Legacy won the Kentucky Derby and the Preakness and was headed for the Triple Crown. Lord Rochester's horse, Millions to Spare, the half brother of Leopold's Legacy, also proved to be a champion."

"If only Texas Tea were registered," Devon mused sadly. She drank some of her bitter. "So what happens now?"

"I need to call my folks and my brother and give them the good news, that it looks like I've found the source of the fraud. If Texas Tea proves to be Leopold's Legacy's sire, as well as Millions to Spare's, we won't have any trouble convincing the Jockey Association we had no intent to misrepresent and that we were the victims of fraud, just as Lord Rochester was. We'll still have to return all our winnings from Leopold's Legacy, but at least we can get our family's good name and reputation back."

"And ours will be ruined completely. You're talking now about my brother's possible involvement in murder."

Brent rotated the handle of the half-pint mug in a semi-circle. "I'm sorry, Devon. I wish this didn't have to happen at your family's expense. But I don't know any way around it, or any way to keep your family's name out of it."

She hung her head. "I don't understand why Nolan would do something so stupid, so disgraceful. It's not going to be easy for Mother."

She had admitted her mother was a cold, self-absorbed woman, yet Devon still worried about the effect a scandal would have on her. It made Brent realize once again how important a mother's love was. As unworthy as Sarah Hunter was, Devon still sought her approval. It reminded him all too poignantly how much his girls needed the love and guidance of a mother.

"Don't underestimate her," Brent said, remembering his own mother's assessment of the ailing widow. "She's had to endure a lot, and she's done it with grace and dignity. She'll get through this, too. She'll need your help and support, of course, but I suspect shouldering this together will help bring you closer."

Devon gazed at him sadly, but there was a spark of hope in her eyes. "You think so?"

He interlaced his fingers with hers. "You're stronger than you think you are, sweetheart. That's one of the reasons I love you."

They sat there, fingers entwined, saying nothing, except with their eyes, until the publican's wife brought their food, the day's special. Crown of lamb, mashed potatoes and green peas. He devoured all of his. She barely touched hers, claiming not to be hungry, until the innkeeper offered syllabub for dessert.

"I tried calling Andrew and my folks from our room earlier," Brent said when they finally slipped out of the booth, "but I couldn't get a signal on my cell phone there. Let me see if I can get one outside."

"I'll wait for you upstairs," she said, as she started moving toward the door to the enclosed staircase.

He grabbed her wrist and stood over her. "We'll get through this, Devon. Together."

She gave him a wan smile, one without joy.

He watched her mount the stairs to the first floor. When she was out of his sight, he turned and went outside into the cold, damp night air and opened his cell phone.

Twenty-One

Back in their room, Devon finished unpacking the few clothes she'd brought with her. She'd been astonished by Brent's announcement this morning that he wanted to come down to this tiny village. The decision seemed to have come out of nowhere. She'd asked him why, but he'd been evasive about details, saying only he'd received a report that he would find something of interest here.

Where and when had he got this information? The two of them had been inseparable since breakfast the morning before. Inseparable in a very literal sense. The memory of their lovemaking still warmed her and made her blush, even in private. They'd done things that, even if she'd thought of them on her own, she'd never expected to actually experience. But with Brent there seemed to be no boundaries to his willingness to please—and be pleased.

There hadn't been any cell phone calls in her presence,

so how had he received this latest tip, if that's what he was reacting to? Or had he been planning to come here all along and just hadn't told her? Either way, it indicated he'd withheld information from her, which could only mean one thing—he didn't trust her. Did he think she had something to do with the horse-breeding fraud? Or was he simply fearful of her passing word along to her brother that the American was closing in on him?

She had just put her case in the corner at the far side of the bed when there was a knock on the door. Had Brent forgot his key?

Smiling, she swung the door open and was about to chide him for his carelessness, but the words never made it past her lips.

"You look eager to see me, my dear. How nice," Charles said with a grin that made her cringe. Without waiting for an invitation, he pushed his way into the room and closed the door firmly behind him.

Frightened by his looming presence in the confined space, Devon backed up and inadvertently fell into a sitting position on the bed. She ought to scream, but shock and fear prevented her from uttering a sound, at least for the first few seconds.

"What are you doing here?" she demanded at last.

"Poor, naive Devon. It's one of the things that make you so attractive, you know, that sweet innocence of yours. Except you're not completely innocent, are you? That's all right. I'm sure there are still things I can teach you."

"Get out. Mr. Preston will be here—"

He smirked. "Your friend is busy trying to establish a cell phone connection. He'll be engaged for some time. We need to talk."

"We have nothing to say to each other. I said, get out."

He studied her with contempt. "You had better listen, my dear, if you know what's good for you. I understand you and your American friend have found Texas Tea, the ringer your brother owned, which he sold when he realized the game was up. It would have been better for everybody concerned if he'd put the horse down. Nolan's going to prison now, thanks to you and your nosey yank. But that's as it should be. After all, your brother stole a great deal of money, didn't he? The only question now is whether your mater will end up being incarcerated, as well."

"My mother?" Devon pulled herself to her feet. Where the hell was Brent?

Charles leaned his shoulders against the front of the highboy and laughed. "I thought that might get your attention."

"What are you talking about? My mother has nothing to do with this. How dare you make such a ludicrous insinuation?"

"Oh, my dear," he said softly as if he really cared. "You haven't figured that part out yet, have you? She's been in on it from the inception. The mastermind behind the scheme. She had to talk your brother—"

"I don't believe you." Her voice shook. "It's all lies, lies—no one would ever believe— My mother would never—"

"You think not?" The self-satisfied expression on his face was utterly confident and terrifying. Dread shivered through her and left her shaking. "You don't have to take my word for it," Charles went on smugly. "I have proof. Her own words." He reached into his coat pocket and removed a small device which Devon recognized immediately as a voice recorder. He held it up. "Listen to this. Listen very carefully, then tell me if your dear mum sounds so bloody innocent."

He pressed a button. Nothing happened for several seconds, then Devon heard her mother's soft, ladylike voice.

"Get rid of it immediately, Nolan. I don't care how much you like the horse or how much money you think it can bring in. Keeping it is much too dangerous. You must dispose of it at once."

"Mother, you don't understand." Nolan's voice.

"I understand better than you realize. You've done very well with Apollo's Ice, but it's time to stop. If you don't, we'll lose everything. You must get rid of him promptly."

Devon sank onto the bed. There was more, but she heard only bits and pieces of it, as she covered her face in horror. This couldn't be happening. This had to be a trick. But the voice was her mother's, no mistaking it, and what the woman was saying was indisputable.

Uncovering her face but unable to look up at the man looming over her, Devon asked, "What do you want?"

"I think you know. I can no longer protect your brother. You have uncovered the evidence against him yourself, but I can keep this evidence of your mother's involvement in fraud and murder out of the hands of the authorities and the press. At least the old girl will be able to live out her remaining years as Viscountess Kestler, the tragic, reclusive dowager of Morningfield Manor, Cambridgeshire, and Pathwatch Hall, London. While you, my dear, will be the Duchess of Camberg. It's a fair bargain, when you consider the alternative."

"You're mad." Or worse, evil.

He chuckled, as if her statement was all in jest and her heart wasn't breaking.

"Leave now," he said harshly. "I don't want you spending another night with him."

"But…I can't just walk out on him." It was a ridiculous argument and she knew it.

"He's ruined you and your family, Devon. I can't imagine why you would want to stay with him. He has nothing to offer you, and I have everything. The Robinett name is prestigious. If you want the Hunter name to remain honorable, you'll do as I say. You'll like being called Duchess, I promise you."

"Get out," she said with all the force she could muster, and it might have been an impressive display of strength, if her voice hadn't been choked and tears weren't already cascading down her cheeks.

"Yes, I'll leave now," he replied nonchalantly. "I expect to see you on the road—alone—within the next twenty minutes."

Brent was frustrated when he couldn't get a signal outside the inn. He returned inside and questioned the publican about cell phone service and was told a local tower was being repaired. If Brent walked about a hundred meters down the lane toward the main road, he should be able to pick up a signal.

He did so but received no answer on his brother's cell phone. He dialed the landline number of the office. Lucie Ann, his part-time secretary, said Andrew's cell phone was sitting on the charger in the office and he was on his way to see their banker in Louisville. Brent could probably reach him there in about an hour. She furnished the number.

Brent then tried to contact his folks. This time he received an out-of-area message. Zero for two. He pictured Devon's face when she left him to go upstairs. As satisfying as the day had been for him, it had turned into a disaster for her. Instinct compelled him to go to her, hold her, comfort her, but another sense told him she needed a little more time alone to sort out what she'd learned, to come to grips with it before she would be able to accept comfort. Procrastinating, he tried his parents' number again, got the same irritating message and finally returned to the inn, climbed the stairs to their room.

She was manhandling her suitcase, trying to force it closed.

"What's going on?" He approached her and saw her face was tearstained, her eyes bloodshot. He'd never seen her like this before.

"I'm leaving." She sat on the lid and managed to snap the latch shut.

"Devon—"

"I'm sorry I ever met you. You've ruined my life. And my brother's. And my mother's."

"Devon, please. Slow down. Think this through. You know what you're saying isn't fair. If anyone's to blame, it's Nolan."

"Sure, blame it all on him."

He put his hand on her shoulder to turn her to face him, but she yanked away with such violence it was as if he'd slapped her. He immediately backed off.

"Devon, calm down. Please. For heaven's sake. I know things look bad, but—"

"Bad?" she shouted at him. "Bad? My brother is going to be charged with felony fraud and God knows what else.

My mother will probably die of the shock and humiliation, and I'll never be able to raise my head in society again. Can it get worse, Brent? If it can, don't tell me."

She grabbed the coat she'd tossed on the only easy chair in the small room, threw it over her shoulder and made for the door.

He stood in her path, which, considering the small size of the room, wasn't difficult, and peered down at her.

"You knew what the stakes were when we set out this morning. Why, all of a sudden, are you so incensed?"

"Get out of my way, Brent."

They stared at each other for several seconds. He hated the pain he saw in her eyes, pain he knew he'd put there. This agony... Was it the social ostracism she was afraid of? He didn't think so. He couldn't remember her ever appearing impressed with her title. Or anyone else's for that matter.

"I love you, Devon. Don't you know that?"

The words seemed to infuriate her all the more. She shoved past him, fumbled to open the door with her free hand, pushed rather than pulled it and started hyperventilating.

Again, he tried to touch her, to calm her.

"No," she snarled. "Keep your hands off me."

He closed his eyes for a second, reached around her and opened the door. Then he stood there as she stormed out and ran down the stairs.

Twenty-Two

Brent followed her and reached the bottom step in time to see her ram her way through the front door. He charged out after her, arriving in the dark car park in time to hear the Austin start up, the engine race angrily, then gravel ping as she skidded down the narrow lane to the macadam byroad. He stood, hands raised, heart pounding, and watched helplessly as the taillights disappeared.

He was stranded without transportation. Most of his clothes were back at Morningfield Manor, but none of that mattered. What was important was that she'd left him. Alone. Abandoned.

Climbing the stairs, he asked himself what he had done wrong, what he could have done differently. It wasn't as if Devon hadn't known what was at stake when they'd started out on this adventure together almost a week earlier, or that he'd forced her participation. She'd volunteered without any encouragement from him. Finding Texas Tea, seeing the stallion that was a double for Apollo's Ice, must have finally brought home to her the depth of her brother's criminal behavior. Brent tried to imagine what his reaction would be if he learned that Andrew or Robbie had committed grand larceny. The very idea made him shudder.

Another hour went by before he was finally able to get hold of Andrew at the bank in Louisville.

"I found him."

"Who?" Andrew asked.

The yelp on the other end of the line when Brent explained had him holding the phone instrument away from his ear. It was the best news he could have delivered, yet now his victory felt hollow.

"You're sure?" Andrew demanded.

"As sure as I can be," Brent replied, trying to match his brother's jubilant mood. He deserved to feel the joy, he told himself, but without Devon the satisfaction felt false. "A blood sample went out by FedEx to the Jockey Association about five hours ago. I'm told it'll get there late tomorrow your time. I'd appreciate it if you would alert them to be on the watch for it and give it priority."

"You don't have to ask me to do that, Brent," Andrew said with a lighthearted chuckle. "It automatically went to the top of my to-do list. Knowing how much they're interested in the outcome of this mess, I don't suppose I'll have to twist any arms. Okay, give me the details."

Twenty minutes later, Andrew asked if Brent had told their parents yet.

"I haven't been able to get hold of them."

"They're in an area with poor cell reception, but I've

got a landline number for them. Wait a minute, let me find it. Here it is. Ready to copy?"

A few minutes later, as Brent was about to hang up, Andrew said, "Ya done good, Brent. How's Devon handling this? The folks sure seemed to like her. Said she's a real looker, too."

"She walked out," he answered, trying to sound matter-of-fact about it, "convinced I've ruined her life."

Andrew's tone became more solicitous. "If she cares about you as much as the folks seem to think she does, Brent, she'll be back. Give her time to calm down. Poor kid. This has been a rough day for her."

"I'd like to wring her brother's neck," Brent replied, "for a couple of reasons."

He called the number in northern England and was connected to his parents' room. Before he could relay the good news, however, he found himself on the phone with the twins. They were bubbly with stories of their adventures. They'd seen castles and knights in shining armor, visited a coal mine—as if there were none in Kentucky— and had gone to a concert for young people.

He was breathless just listening to them ramble on and wished he could give them both big hugs. He wasn't surprised when they asked to speak to Devon so they could tell her all about their adventures, too. He was forced to say she wasn't there, that she was running errands. They were disappointed and made him promise to have her call them, as soon as she came back. He would, he said, but maybe not tonight. Finally, after saying goodbye to the girls for the fourth or fifth time— he'd lost count—he was allowed to talk to his father.

"I found him," he said, "the ringer."

Another twenty minutes went by as he repeated the story of how they'd found Texas Tea.

"How is Devon handling the situation?" his mother asked. She'd been listening in on the extension in the bedroom.

He told them about her fleeing.

"What are you going to do now?" his father asked.

"I'll take the train into London in the morning and check with the lab there to make sure they got the sample. Andrew is asking the Jockey Association to give priority to the one I sent them. As soon as we get the DNA results back, if they're positive, the next step will be to go to the police and swear out a complaint against Nolan."

"We'll meet you in London tomorrow," Thomas said. "Don't know what time, yet, but probably early afternoon. It'll take a few days to get the test results back, but when we do, I have the name of a good lawyer...solicitor we can consult before we approach the authorities. We want to do this right."

"I agree," Brent said. "By the numbers. We want to make sure Nolan Hunter, the Viscount Kestler, doesn't wriggle his noble arse through any loopholes."

"You've done good work, son. I'm sorry things haven't worked out for you and Devon, but you've made me proud, the way you've handled all this."

His father's praise should have consoled him, but all he could think of was Devon's tearstained face and the look of abject misery in her chocolate-brown eyes.

Brent arrived at Paddington Station before noon on Tuesday and took a taxi to the hotel. The clerk at the desk told him his luggage from Morningfield Manor had arrived an hour earlier and had already been deposited in his room.

The news didn't raise his spirits.

He went upstairs, unpacked, hoping to find a note from Devon—there wasn't any—called the lab where he'd had the blood and hair samples couriered and was assured the case was being given highest priority.

The girls arrived while he was in the dining room eating a late lunch. Suddenly the world didn't seem nearly so gloomy.

Tuesday afternoon, he and his father talked to Andrew on the phone and spoke to Hugh, who kept thanking Brent for tracking down Texas Tea. On Wednesday morning they had a productive conversation with a solicitor who specialized in equine matters. Brent and his father conferred over drinks later that day with an English representative of the Jockey Association at his club in the city.

On Thursday, Jenna took her granddaughters to Madame Tussaud's.

Twice on Tuesday, three times on Wednesday and twice more on Thursday, Brent called Morningfield Manor and asked for Devon. Each time he was politely told she was not available, and each time the butler who answered the phone was unable to say when she might be. Brent was tempted to call Pathwatch Hall to see if she was there, but each time he hung up before completing the connection. He didn't know what he would say if Devon's mother came on the line. Did she know what was going on? Had she known, as Jenna speculated, what was transpiring around her all the time?

Brent and his family dined together every evening. The girls watched a different DVD every night.

And Brent waited.

At 4:15 p.m. on Thursday, Brent's cell phone rang.

"It's a hit," Andrew said. "Texas Tea is the sire of Leopold's Legacy and Millions to Spare."

That afternoon, accompanied by their solicitor, Brent and his father swore out formal complaints against Nolan Hunter, the Viscount Kestler, for grand larceny and a host of other related charges, including conspiracy to defraud. A warrant was signed for his arrest, and an hour later the nobleman was taken into custody at his London flat.

Twenty-Three

Friday, January 23

Brent flew back to Kentucky with his parents and twin daughters and was received at Quest like a returning hero. His grandfather, Hugh Preston, met him with tears in his eyes and thanked him for saving the family's name and honor. It was an unusually emotional display for the eighty-six-year-old founder of the Quest dynasty, and one that moved Brent as deeply as any event in his life.

Ten days later the Jockey Association, working diligently with local and regional racing commissions, lifted the ban on Quest Stables. Within hours, owners began bringing their horses back for training. The current breeding season was only just beginning, so Brent was able to negotiate enough contracts, albeit at discounted rates, to reverse the negative cash flow they'd been plagued with for more than six months, and Andrew was able to hire back many of the employees he'd been forced to lay off.

"It'll take upwards of a year to get all the legal details worked out," Andrew told the family at dinner one evening, "and we'll still have to pay back all our race earnings from Leopold's Legacy, but at least we'll be operating in the black again, thanks to Brent."

"I didn't do it alone," his brother replied, embarrassed by the adulation he'd been getting from family, friends and staff.

He couldn't have done it without Devon's help, either, and the knowledge that he'd saved his family by destroying hers hung like an albatross around his neck. He'd made a series of attempts to contact her, but they'd all failed. His telephone messages went unanswered; his letters were returned as undeliverable.

"We've filed a civil claim for reimbursement of direct expenses against the Hunter estate," Thomas reminded Andrew, "since it was through the viscount's fraud that we incurred the financial losses. Then there's the matter of punitive damage for the harm done to our good name and reputation."

"What do you hear from England?" Jenna asked Brent.

He had one private contact over there, Brice Halpern, the head groom at Morningfield Manor. They spoke by cell phone every week, sometimes more than once. Halpern was grateful to Brent for not identifying him as the source of information about Texas Tea. For sure, he said, he would have been sacked without references and probably marked as a disloyal and untrustworthy employee, despite his more than thirty-five years of service.

"Lady Kestler posted a quarter-million-pound bond to get her son released from custody," Brent said. "Wisely he's refused to make any public statements about the charges against him. His mother and sister have followed suit."

"How is the old lady handling the situation?" asked Robbie, the youngest Preston son and Quest trainer.

"According to my source, she's had several private meetings with Nolan, but no one seems to know exactly what they've talked about. If she's upset with him, she's giving no indication of it in public or in private."

"Stiff upper lip and all that, eh?" Robbie commented cynically.

"Do you think she was aware of what was going on from the beginning?" Melanie's fiancé, Marcus Vasquez, asked his prospective mother-in-law.

Jenna shook her head. "My guess is that at some point she figured out something was amiss, but I seriously doubt she was a party to it. She's a very proud woman. I can't imagine her getting involved in a criminal conspiracy."

"Coughing up a quarter million pounds, and hiring one of the most prestigious and expensive legal teams in England seems to prove your theory that she controls the family purse strings," Brent added.

"What do you hear about Devon?" his mother asked.

Brent took a deep breath. He hated thinking about the beautiful young woman he'd fallen in love with having to cope with all this without him, even if he was—at least in part—the source of the pain.

"She's apparently been keeping regular company with Charles Robinett. They've been observed at various social functions in the past month."

"Unbelievable." Thomas snorted. "If he's really the

bastard she made him out to be, she's got to be a masochist to go back to him. Then again, I suppose we have to give her high marks for fortitude. With the number of charges against her brother growing almost daily, and the Hunter name being dragged through the mud by the media, it can't be easy for her to mix in society."

"I'm sure setting her hand on the arm of a duke keeps tongues from wagging, at least to her face," Melanie suggested with uncharacteristic sarcasm.

"Yet Nolan refuses to give an explanation for what he did," Thomas observed.

"Money, of course," remarked Marcus. "Isn't that enough? We are talking about millions."

Brent didn't disagree. "I just wonder if there's more to it than that."

"May I have your attention, please?" Andrew tapped the side of his wineglass with his fork. "I have an announcement to make."

Everybody stopped and looked at him.

"I received a telephone call this afternoon from George Witherspoon, the head of the Thoroughbred registry in Australia. He and a group of his friends have asked me to stand for president of the International Thoroughbred Racing Federation."

"Wow!" Melanie exclaimed. "Awesome."

"Congratulations," Robbie concurred.

"It's about time a Preston set that outfit straight," Hugh said, all smiles.

Jenna leaned over and kissed her eldest son on the cheek. Thomas shook his hand.

"That's wonderful news, Andrew," Brent said. "I'm really proud of you."

"It also means you'll be taking over here as general manager, Brent," Andrew said with a proud smile. "Well deserved, too. No one's more dedicated to Quest Stables than you are, and I mean that with complete respect for everyone at this table. You know how Quest works and you're totally committed to its success and integrity. It's in your hands now, where it deserves to be."

Taking over Quest was something Brent had long dreamed of, but now he felt strangely humbled—though not daunted—by the prospect. "What about you?" he asked his brother.

"There are no declared candidates for president from Europe or North America right now," Andrew replied, "but there will be, and I'll use my proxies to campaign for me there. My main opponent, according to Witherspoon, is a guy by the name of Jacko Bullock in Australia, so it looks like I'll be spending most of my time Down Under."

Suddenly the men at the table were standing and everyone was applauding the two brothers. They looked at each other and grinned.

But as happy and fulfilling as the moment was for Brent, there was still an unfinished matter he had to take care of.

Twenty-Four

Monday, February 1

Remembering Katie's reaction to Briar Hills Academy for Girls, Brent decided not to tell his daughters he was going back to England, only that he was going to be away for a few days. Then he reconsidered. It was likely the twins would find out where he was, and hiding his whereabouts from them would make matters worse. So he came clean.

"I'm going back to London for a few days," he told them at breakfast the next morning.

"Are you taking us with you?" Rhea wanted to know.

"Not this time, sweet pea," he said. "Last time was a vacation. This time it's strictly business, then I'll be back."

"Is it about horses?"

He felt confident telling this fib. "Yes, I have some details I need to take care of."

"Are you going to see Devon?" Katie asked.

"I might." He certainly hoped so.

"Tell her we miss her. We wish she was here with us."

He smiled. "I sure will, pumpkin."

Luckily, he was able to snag a seat for Wednesday morning through Chicago that got him into Heathrow late that evening.

To his amazement, he slept most of the way across the Atlantic, maybe because he was by himself with no responsibilities and because he knew exactly what he was after—or, more specifically, who. He took a taxi to the same hotel he'd stayed at before, having called ahead for reservations. The staff greeted him by name.

An invigorating shower and change of clothes, and he was on his way.

Thanks to Brice Halpern, he had a good idea where he'd find Charles Robinett.

L'Exquisite was a prestigious and fashionable "event" in the city. Wednesday, however, wasn't one of its busy nights, especially during the low tourist season, so he had little difficulty buying his way inside. A discreet word and a generous show of appreciation to the maître d' revealed that His Grace, the Duke of Camberg, had just finished dinner and was about to retire to the game room.

That put Brent at a slight disadvantage. He'd never been much of a gambler. He'd played poker in college a few times and never won much. The good news was that he'd never lost much, either. He entered the casino area of the nightclub. Most of the tables appeared to be full, or nearly so, which suited him. In the far corner of the room was a bar. He casually migrated there and ordered a gin and tonic.

Surveying the casino, he finally spied the duke at a baccarat table. Maybe later he would join him. It might be fun to see if His Lordship would be spooked by his presence, but for the time being he was content to watch from afar.

He sipped his drink and studied the man.

Robinett played his cards with easy familiarity but, at least for the three hands Brent observed, not very well. A fourth hand was being dealt when Brent's eyes were automatically drawn to the doorway at the far end of the vast room.

There she was. Petite, almost delicate looking, wearing a perfectly tailored, low-cut, coppery dress. Multi strands of pearls decorated her exposed skin. Her luxuriant chestnut hair was swept up and held in place with antique combs. The style was retro and yet classically in vogue.

Devon was stunningly beautiful. She stood for a moment in the doorway, regarding the assembly. Brent slipped easily behind a potted palm, able to glimpse her without being seen. Her eyes settled on Charles, and she wove her way across the room toward him.

Brent was too far away to hear what was said, but it was obvious from the way she greeted him that they were together.

The hand over, Charles tossed in his cards and stood up. He'd lost again. Devon came up beside him, allowed him to place his arm around her waist and smiled at the people in their circle as he kissed her on the temple. They made their leisurely way toward the door of the casino.

Brent was devastated. Clearly she hadn't spotted him,

which was probably as well. He'd seen her acting spontaneously familiar with the man who had been stalking her for two years.

Had Charles been telling the truth when he claimed their separation had been nothing more than a temporary lovers' quarrel, a silly spat that he had indulged? Devon didn't look like a woman who was afraid of the man holding her. If anything, the gleam in her eyes as she gazed up at him after he'd kissed her said the opposite.

Brent realized he'd been bamboozled, hoodwinked, taken in by another Hunter. First Nolan, then his sister. Even their mother, if Jenna's assessment had been correct.

He finished his drink and exited the casino. In the central lobby he heard music coming from the ballroom that made up the other third of the nightclub. He supposed Devon and Charles were in there dancing, but Brent chose not to find out. The last thing he needed now was to see her in the duke's arms on the dance floor.

Outside it was raining. He stood under the overhang for several minutes before the valet was able to hail a taxi to take him back to his hotel. There he wandered into the private bar and ordered another gin and tonic. Then he went upstairs, crawled into bed and went to sleep almost immediately.

The next morning he called the solicitor his father had engaged and made an appointment. He still felt strangely like a zombie, a robot, later in the day as he sat across from the lawyer and inquired into the progress of the case.

"Nolan Hunter is out on bail," the balding, bespectacled man informed him, "and still residing at his flat in Mayfair. I can tell you, Mr. Preston, that the Crown's case against him is airtight and grows stronger every day."

"Has he offered any explanation, other than greed, for his actions?"

"None. He hasn't even copped to greed. He neither acknowledges nor disputes the mounting column of evidence against him and refuses to offer any explanation whatsoever for his actions."

"Is that unusual?" Brent asked.

The man leaned back and laced his fingers across his narrow waist. "Initial silence isn't unheard of, but in my experience it most commonly is practiced by career criminals who are familiar enough with the system not to be easily intimidated by it. That tactic typically ends when they get whatever concession they want in return for speaking out. Some, too, simply enjoy it as a game to frustrate authorities. Eventually they all talk, even if only in an attempt to prove how clever they are."

"Any idea why Nolan Hunter hasn't?"

"None." The solicitor shook his head. "It's quite baffling, actually, since he's only hurting himself."

That evening, Brent returned to L'Exquisite, only to learn Charles wasn't there.

Brice had mentioned two other places that the duke frequented. The first was a private club; despite Brent's best efforts at bribery, he was unable to gain admission.

The second was public and he had no difficulty getting in. No casino in this club, only a dining room and lounge. He wasn't hungry, having eaten a couple of hours earlier at the hotel, so once again he made his way to the bar.

There were only a few couples on the dance floor, gyrating to the music of a small combo. One of them was Devon and Charles.

She was wearing a more casual outfit tonight, an

above-the-knee brown-and-gold skirt and cream silk blouse. It was too revealing in Brent's estimation, but there was no doubt she was beautiful in it. Every male and many of the females were watching them. She and Charles were also dancing too close. They looked like lovers. The very thought cut like a knife into Brent's heart.

The tempo morphed to a slow number and as they glided across the floor, Charles bent his head and kissed her on the lips. In the middle of the dance floor. In front of everybody.

Brent was at once sick to his stomach and hot with rage. He would have liked to march out there, plant his hand on the duke's shoulder, spin him around and ram a solid fist in his arrogant face. Doing so would no doubt result only in his being arrested for assault and possibly spending an ignoble night in jail. He was about to turn and leave, satisfied he'd seen enough, when he caught a fleeting glimpse of Devon's face. It wasn't one of elation or pleasure at being kissed, but rather one of disgust and misery. Then the expression was gone.

Surely he hadn't seen it. Surely it was only the shadowy light playing tricks on him, mirroring what he felt rather than what he saw. He ordered another drink and continued to observe them.

Brent studied the duke. Was it only his imagination, or did the man look more dissolute than when they'd met a few weeks earlier at the Archers' Ball? Could no one else discern that the possessiveness in the aristocrat's muddy hazel eyes was that of a cruel man rather than a lover?

As the slow number droned on, Charles tightened his hold on the woman in his arms. To Brent, the gesture seemed calculated to taunt the other men in the room, demonstrating that she was his alone, while at the same time humiliating her as nothing more than a possession, an object to be toyed with.

This time, when Charles pulled her closer, Devon tried to push him away. There was nothing playful in the way he grabbed her back, slamming her against his chest.

She said something Brent couldn't hear, but reading her lips, he was sure it was, "Charles, let me go, or I'll scream."

The duke narrowed his eyes at her, then grinned with spiteful merriment. "Of course, my dear."

He loosened his grip and she slid out of his embrace and walked off the dance floor toward the ladies' room. Brent watched her disappear around the corner, then refocused his attention on the duke. Camberg made for the bar. Even before he had reached it, the bartender was pouring him another drink.

With the duke's back to the crowd, Brent went out into the lobby and sat on one of the settees along the wall between the men's and ladies' rooms. Several minutes went by before Devon emerged. She halted in her tracks and let out a startled mew of surprise when she saw him.

"Hello, Devon." He had his legs casually crossed as he gazed up at her. She was beautiful. He wanted desperately to hold her in his arms.

"What are you doing here?" she demanded almost breathlessly.

"Not a very friendly greeting."

"I didn't ask you to come."

"No, you left me. I'm still trying to figure out why."

"I told you."

"You told me nonsense."

"You must leave. At once. If he finds you here—"

"What will happen, Devon?"

"Brent, please," she begged, and for the first time he heard abject fear rather than anger in her voice. "It's far more complicated than you realize."

He rose to his feet and approached her. "Then explain it to me."

She backed away. Her eyes teared up. "I can't."

"Can't or won't?" he challenged.

"Please don't interfere. If you do, he'll have my mother arrested, and—" She sniffled and her words caught.

Brent moved forward to put his arms around her, but she turned her back on him. He refused to accept defeat, so the only alternative was anger.

"What is all this about? You're talking nonsense."

"Apollo's Ice," she hissed. "He'll have my mother arrested for being part of the fraud."

"Was she?"

Devon spun around. "Of course not, but he has evidence he can use. Go, Brent. Please. There's nothing you can do. Hurry."

"Devon," Camberg's voice called with annoyance, as he came through the lounge doorway. "How long—" He stopped when he saw Brent standing beside her. "What the bloody hell are you doing here? Devon, go inside. Now. We'll talk about this later. First, I must deal with this American meddler."

Brent grinned. No proxies this time.

Camberg came up to him. He was as tall as Brent and at least thirty pounds heavier, but he'd also been drinking heavily and wasn't nearly as fit as his opponent in the best circumstances.

Brent refused to back off, though Devon did take a step behind him.

"I told you to go inside," Camberg snarled at her.

She didn't move.

"Is something wrong, milord?" a male voice asked from an office door across from the lounge.

"This foreigner is interfering with the lady."

"He isn't," Devon protested, surprising both men. "We were just talking."

"Do you want me to call someone, Your Grace?" the man asked Camberg.

"I'll take care of this," the duke replied, not looking at him. Then, without warning, he raised his right fist and swung at Brent's face.

Brent ducked and easily sidestepped the swing, so that Camberg went tottering forward into empty space. Brent made eye contact with the other man. "You're a witness. He swung at me first."

In a few seconds, Camberg regained his balance, came around and threw another punch, this one even more poorly aimed and coordinated. Brent planted a fist solidly in the man's flabby middle, doubling him over.

Devon screamed.

The other man stood there, transfixed, uncertain for several seconds, then he scurried into his office and picked up the phone.

Twenty-Five

"Come on," Brent said, as he grabbed Devon by the arm and escorted her toward the club's entrance.

By now club patrons were emerging from the neighboring rooms. Charles regained his feet, shook off the two men who had come to his assistance, and lurched toward Brent and Devon. Brent shielded her with his body and blocked the duke's advance. The people around them gawked like spectators at a traffic accident, curious but unwilling to get involved.

"Go outside," Brent ordered Devon.

She wanted to argue with him, tell him it was no use. They couldn't run away. Charles would catch up with them, and when he did it would only be worse. But there were so many thoughts stampeding through her head, none of them happy, that the words got jumbled and nothing came out.

"Go outside and get a cab," Brent urged louder. "Hurry."

"Brent—"

"Dammit—" he narrowed his eyes with annoyance but refused to be distracted from the overweight man struggling to regain his breath and composure "—just do it."

She stiffened at his tone. He was acting like Charles. No, that wasn't true. Brent was nothing like Charles. Brent had told her he loved her. Charles never had and she doubted he ever would or could. Brent told her he loved her and she had walked out, run away. The only man who ever...

"I'm going to have you arrested for bloody assault." Charles's raised voice thundered over the music still blasting from the band in the other room and the murmur of the crowd that had gathered.

"Go," Brent barked. "We'll talk about this later. Just get out of here."

Reluctantly, she ran toward the entrance of the club. No one had ever stood up to Charles the way Brent was now and she wanted to see what was going to happen. The doorman held the door for her.

It was raining hard.

"I need a taxi—immediately," she said to the outside man, who was huddled under the short canopy.

"Coming right up, miss."

He expanded a large black umbrella and blew a whistle. A cab that had been loitering a few doors down pulled to the curb. The valet had just opened the back door for Devon when Brent came bounding out of the nightclub, thrust some crumpled money into the man's hand, grabbed Devon by the elbow and practically shoved her into the grumbling vehicle. He ordered the driver to get a move on. Pronto. Seconds later they were rolling down the rain-slicked street on their way to his hotel.

"What are you doing here?" Devon demanded, her heart pounding in both happiness and fear.

He grinned over at her. "Rescuing you."

She ground her teeth. "You are the most impertinent, irresponsible, conceited—"

He reached over and brushed her cheek gently. "I love you, too," he said in a near whisper.

Her heart rose and fell. She couldn't say if the tears that blinded her were of joy or sorrow.

That was the second time he'd told her that, and as glorious as the words sounded, they terrified her even more. So far, protestations of love had brought only misery and helplessness. No, that wasn't completely true. What she'd felt with Brent, what she still felt having him by her side, was anything but misery. But inevitably, she knew, it would follow.

"Don't say that," she murmured.

"Not saying the words won't change anything, Devon." He gazed into her eyes. "Now, tell me what's going on. Why were you with that man?"

They arrived at his hotel. He paid the driver, adding a generous tip, and they got out. Beyond the front door he took her hand and led her toward the lift. She pulled back.

"Where are we going?"

"To my room. We can talk there."

"I shouldn't. When Charles finds out—"

"It won't make any difference," Brent said, shaking his head. "You're not going back to him."

She pulled away. "That's my decision, not yours."

He studied her as they stood in the middle of the lobby. The clerk at the desk feigned indifference. A couple coming out of the bar glanced at them as they passed by.

"I would never force you to do anything, Devon. I hope you know that. I'm asking you to come up to my room so we can talk. If you would prefer to not be alone with me, we can go into the bar and talk there. And if you want to turn your back and walk out on me again, you can do that, too. The decision is yours," he said softly. "This time I won't come after you again."

She could all but feel her face fall. He was so serious, so solemn, and she knew without a doubt that he meant every word he said.

Would it be weakness on her part to give in to him? Would going with him be an act of surrender if being with him was what she really wanted? She needed time to think, but she didn't have time. What she also knew was that she didn't have the strength to push him away again, either, that living without him wasn't living at all, merely enduring existence. She could withstand any pain with him holding her hand, but she couldn't bear the agony of not having him close to her.

"All right," she said, "your room."

He didn't take her hand this time as he continued to lead her to the lift. She stood at his side, as they ascended. He didn't reach out for her but maintained his distance. The only sound was the whine of the cables overhead and the heavy beating of her heart.

Halfway down the upstairs hall, he stopped at a door, inserted a key card and held the door open for her to precede him inside.

"Can I get you something to drink?" he asked in the most casual way, but he didn't fool her. He was no more at ease than she was.

"Maybe some sparkling water, if there is any."

He found a bottle of Vichy, pried off the cap, poured it into a glass and handed it to her. He opened a second bottle for himself.

"Now, will you please tell me what's going on?"

He watched her struggle to put her thoughts into words.

"That night in Dorset," she began, "the reason I left…was because Charles showed up at the room and told me unless I returned to him he would have my mother arrested along with my brother for the Apollo's Ice fraud, that she conspired with him—"

"Why would you believe that if it isn't true?"

"Because he had a voice recording of them talking about it on the telephone."

Brent didn't think highly of Sarah Hunter. He'd come to agree with his mother's assessment that the elderly woman was selfish and manipulative. One conclusion he hadn't drawn, however, was that she was criminally dishonest. Perhaps she was, but he had at present no reason to think so.

"And you found this evidence credible?" he asked.

"If it were presented to anyone the way it was presented to me…yes. I found it credible. That's not the same as my believing it was true. I was afraid she could be charged and—"

"Your mother is tougher than you've given her credit for. Look at the way she's handled your brother's arrest. Haven't the events since then proved that?"

She flashed an angry glare at him. "I didn't know that at the time, did I?"

He was tempted to say she should have, but that kind of accusation wouldn't accomplish anything. Sarah Hunter had spent years cultivating the impression that she was a frail and delicate creature. Physically she was no doubt weak and vulnerable, unless that, too, was an affectation.

But as he considered the complex relationship between the woman and her two children, other thoughts crowded in on him, as well. Brent had suspected for some time that Nolan was behind the fraud, and if Jenna was correct that the elder Lady Kestler controlled the family's money, Nolan would have had a sound financial reason for perpetuating the hoax of Apollo's Ice's fertility.

What Brent hadn't considered was that Nolan might not be alone in masterminding the scam. From what Devon just told him, it was now clear Charles knew about it. Which raised an interesting question. Why would a duke tolerate such a hoax in a field in which he was an active player? Could it be that he actively participated in it?

Brent gulped down the water in his glass, rose to his feet, grabbed his overcoat from the rack by the door and draped it over Devon's shoulders. She'd left her wrap at the nightclub.

"Come on," he said.

"Where are we going?" She sounded totally bewildered, and perhaps scared.

"To see your brother."

"At this hour? It's nearly midnight."

"Then we have a good chance of finding him at home."

He ushered her to the door. She pulled back. In hesitation, he noted, not refusal.

"I'll explain it to you on the way," he said. "Trust me on this, Devon. I can't promise it will make things easier for Nolan, but it might at least give us an explanation of what's been going on and identify the real villain."

Nolan met them at the door of his flat wearing a silk dressing gown and a scowl. The sight of Brent with his sister didn't improve his disposition.

"What the hell is he doing here?" His tone was one of annoyance and resignation.

"I need to ask you some questions," Brent said.

"And why in the blue bloody blazes should I answer them?"

"Let us in," Devon ordered. She and Brent were still standing in the hallway, Nolan blocking the entrance to his flat. She pushed past him. Brent followed.

More angry than before, Nolan slammed the door behind them. "Go through to the sitting room." But Devon was already heading that way. "Why don't you," he added and trailed along behind.

The room was very much as Brent remembered it from his earlier visit. Tastefully austere. Signed black-and-white abstract etchings in black frames on the stark, white walls. Black leather-and-chrome furniture which he remembered as being remarkably comfortable in spite of its uninviting look. The only color in the room was the wine-red fitted carpet.

Nolan went to the drinks table next to the nearly wall-to-wall window that gave a stunning view of London, the dome of St. Paul's visible in the distance. He poured himself a stiff one but didn't offer the others anything.

"Now," he said, turning to face them. "What the bloody hell do you want?"

"Who's in charge?" Brent asked. "You or Charles?"

The stunned silence didn't last more than a few seconds, but it was enough.

"What are you talking about?"

"Charles," Brent concluded. "The question is, why?"

Nolan went over to one of the armchairs and sat down. "You might as well help yourselves to the bar, because this is going to take a while. And if you think I'm going to serve you like some kind of honored guest, you are out of your flippin' mind."

"I'll take a gin," Devon said to Brent as she glared crossly at her brother.

"Gin?" Her brother rolled his eyes. "So common. Mother would be absolutely appalled."

Brent poured a couple of fingers of Bombay into a small tumbler—drinking liquor without ice still struck him as uncivilized—and handed it over to her. He noticed a bottle of Basil Hayden's Straight Bourbon. At least Nolan had good taste in Kentucky sipping whisky.

"A little over four years ago, I was in a casino," Nolan began after his visitors were seated. "I'm not much of a gambler, lost my limit and was leaving when I ran into Charles. We'd met a few times at racetracks. He seemed like a nice enough chap, but I knew I was out of my league."

"Him being a duke and all," Brent offered.

Devon quirked a brow at him, but her brother seemed not to notice the sarcasm in the remark.

"That was part of it," Nolan continued, "but he was also a much bigger spender than I was able to be. Generous, but I knew I could never reciprocate. That evening I'd had a bit more to drink than I was accustomed to, or at least more than was wise for me. I'd left my Jaguar in a car park down the street, an unattended one. He walked with me. I offered him a lift to wherever he was off to, but he said the friend he planned to visit—I got the impression it was a woman—lived nearby. We shook hands and he went on his way."

Nolan downed most of the drink in his glass, got up and splashed in more, then returned to his chair before proceeding with his narrative.

"I had pulled out of the car park and was driving down the street in the same direction Charles was walking when a man stepped out in front of me. I have no idea where he came from. One moment the way was clear, the next he was in my path. I hit him before his presence had even completely registered."

He took another taste of his whisky.

"I slammed on the brakes, jumped out of the car, bolted around the front and bent over the man. There was no blood, no sign of an injury, but he wasn't moving, either. I had enough presence of mind to check his pulse. He had none. I couldn't believe it. I'd just killed a man in a matter of seconds without even realizing he was there."

"Oh, my God," Devon cried, and covered her face.

"Charles came running up, a cell phone in his hand. Call the police, I told him, but he just stood there, waving the cell phone around, apparently as horrified by the situation as I was. Call the police, I repeated, but he said that would be foolish. It was clearly an accident, but if word of this got out my name would be all over the *Star* in the morning. Viscount Kestler Kills Innocent Pedestrian on Drunken Night Out."

Nolan rose and began to pace, his drink in hand.

"I thought about the repercussions that would follow. Mother would be mortified." He looked at his sister. "So would you. The legal battles and lawsuits would go on for years, draining us of respectability and resources. And it wouldn't bring the poor man back. I hadn't hit him maliciously or even moving very fast, just fast enough to snap his neck, I guess."

"So you fled," Brent commented.

"It was a stupid thing to do. I know that now, but at the time…"

"How long before the blackmail began?" Brent asked.

"Six weeks. There had been a small article in the paper about a homeless man being found dead on Suffix Road, the victim of an apparent hit-and-run. The police said they had a lead on the culprit but refused to disclose any further details. According to them, an arrest was imminent. Needless to say I was terrified. Every time the phone rang, every knock on the door had me shaking. Then the matter seemed to die. Nothing more appeared in the papers. It had not even made it to the evening news on television."

He poured more Scotch into his glass, though he hadn't drunk what was already there.

"Charles came to visit me. All very friendly and concerned. Until he showed me the photo he'd got off his video cell phone. The devices were quite new then. I'd never been much of a geek—is that the right word? But Charles was fascinated by the stuff. I didn't even have a regular cell phone at the time. I suppose I'd heard of videophones, but I thought they were a novelty that would quickly wear off. Who'd be interested in a picture that was little more than the size of a postage stamp?" He snorted and took a slug of his drink. "Well, this picture, after it was blown up, showed me kneeling over the dead man. The image was grainy, but my features were quite distinct, as were the numbers of my car tag."

"What did he want?" Brent asked.

"Money, of course. He's much better at spending it than he is at earning it. I soon discovered he was up to his neck in debt."

That explained Charles's hold over Nolan Hunter, but what about the breeding scam?

"How does Apollo's Ice fit into this?" Brent asked.

Twenty-Six

"Charles knew I was standing Apollo's Ice at stud, and that I was able to command enormous fees for him," Nolan explained. "He wanted a cut, because he had accumulated large gambling debts, which he was unable to pay off."

"Why didn't you just say no?" Devon asked.

"I should have. I know that now. I knew it then, too, but the idea of facing you and Mother and all our friends as someone who had run a man down to death while drunk was too shameful to contemplate."

"And it didn't occur to you that this would not be a onetime request?" Brent asked.

"Charles assured me he had only to get past this one hurdle."

Devon's laugh was bitter and filled with contempt. "I can't believe you were such a stupid fool."

Nolan closed his eyes, took a deep breath and opened

them again. "Each time I paid him he insisted it was the last. Till the next time, of course." He drank more of his whisky.

"Then Apollo suffered a series of systemic infections accompanied by high fevers. I knew the result could be sterility, so I sent a sperm sample off, which confirmed what I suspected. Believe it or not, I felt relieved. I figured I was off the hook. Then Charles presented me with yet another surprise."

"He'd found a look-alike," Brent said.

Nolan nodded. "It seemed utterly impossible for two horses to resemble each other as closely as they did."

"Why didn't you just substitute Texas Tea for Apollo's Ice?" Brent asked, looking at Devon.

"Because they didn't look enough alike to fool anyone who knew them, like the stable lads," Nolan replied, confirming what Brent had previously told her. "The offspring would be convincing in looks, but not the stallion."

"And the DNA registrations?"

"Charles already had an accomplice at the Jockey Association lab. He seems to have them everywhere. That's why he gets away with so much. Everywhere he turns he's got someone willing to cover for him."

"Ross Ingliss," Brent stated.

"Yes," Nolan said, apparently not surprised that Brent knew his name. "He agreed—for a fee, of course—to certify any foal whose blood sample identified its sire as Apollo's Ice."

"Then came the computer glitch," Brent reminded him.

Nolan settled heavily into the chair he had vacated and cupped his whisky glass between his hands. He stared at it for several seconds before he finally looked up. "Until then everything had been going well. Maybe at some time off in the distant future someone would notice that the sire DNA of different foals of Apollo's Ice weren't the same, but that possibility seemed extremely remote, and by then we'd be out of the picture."

"The real danger was getting caught at the time of breeding," Brent suggested.

His eyes unfocused, Nolan nodded. "After Apollo's Ice went sterile, I always sent Neal Caruthers with him as groom. He took frozen sperm we'd collected from Texas Tea with him. The night after the mare had been covered, he'd artificially inseminated her. It's not a difficult procedure for someone who knows what he's doing, and it doesn't take but a few minutes, so there was little danger of getting caught. In fact, he never was."

"Did you know Neal Caruthers died weeks ago in what appears to have been a driving accident in Scotland?"

"I heard about it from one of the stable lads and checked out the notice in the Glasgow paper."

"And it didn't raise any suspicions?"

"Of course it did, and it scared the daylights out of me."

"Did you question Charles about it?"

"I mentioned it to him."

Devon was staring now at her brother, shocked at what she was hearing. "You mentioned it to him?"

"What more could I do?" he asked. "He said it was a pity, but Neal was always a careless driver, that he should have been more careful on those mountain roads. Except the paper had said nothing about a mountain road. That's when I knew he was somehow responsible for Neal's death. Charles wouldn't have done it himself, of course. He never gets his hands dirty with things like that—"

"Like my being attacked at Morningfield Manor," Brent observed.

"Exactly."

Devon jumped to her feet and began striding the floor on the other side of the room, as far away from her brother as she could get. "I can't believe I'm hearing all this," she complained to no one in particular. "I trusted you, Nolan, yet you were willing to marry me off to a man you suspected of murder?"

Wisely, her brother said nothing, just continued to stare blankly in front of him.

Still pacing and seeming to get more angry with every step, Devon asked, "How much is Mother involved in all this?"

"Mother?" Nolan's head shot up. "Not at all. How can you even suggest it? She's selfish and self-absorbed, and God knows she's tightfisted when it comes to anyone but herself, but the idea of getting involved in something like this... Preposterous."

"She went your bail," Devon reminded him.

He laughed. "To save her own face. She didn't want to have her son's forwarding address to be Her Majesty's prison. But she also made me sign a paper agreeing to pay her back for the bail and all the legal expenses—assuming, of course, I get off. Which I won't. I've decided to plead—"

"Charles played the recording of a conversation you and Mother had about Apollo's Ice, in which she told you to get rid of him."

Nolan stared at her from under furrowed brows. "That's impossible. We never had any such conversation."

"It was you and Mother," Devon insisted. "There was no mistaking your voices."

Nolan shook his head. "It's not possible, I tell you. Wait, what exactly did we say?"

Devon recounted the discussion as best she could remember it, including the reference to Apollo's Ice.

Nolan rocked his head back and forth. "I don't believe that man. If he put as much energy and ingenuity into productive work as he does into his criminal activities, he'd be headed for Minister of the Exchequer. He likes technology, I already told you that. He may have glommed several conversations together or be using one I had with Mother when I bought Cavalier Canard, a two-year-old who had fantastic speed but was too unruly to be dependable. I argued that Apollo's Ice had been that way early on, as well, but that he eventually calmed down. She maintained that Cavalier Canard was too dangerous, that I was just lucky Apollo's Ice came through."

Devon ceased her pacing and regarded him thoughtfully. "It's possible. I'd have to hear the recording again, but I think it's possible."

"He's a wily bastard. It's all a game to him."

And if you had said no to him the first time, Brent thought, he would have moved on to find someone else to torture.

"One more question," Brent said to the other man. "Why have you kept quiet about all this? When you were arrested, why didn't you spill the beans, bring the house of cards down on Charles? Why have you been protecting him?"

Nolan returned to his collection of bottles and added another ounce of whisky to his glass. This time he didn't drink it, however. Instead, he leaned against the sideboard and gazed at his sister.

"Because he told me if I didn't keep my mouth shut, he would hurt Devon. Not kill her. Hurt her and see to it she hurt for the rest of her life."

Devon's mouth fell open.

"I wanted to protect you, but I didn't know how," he said to her. "I knew he was capable of following through on his threat. I had to find a way of forestalling him until I could stop him once and for all. My plan is to kill him, but as you know I'm neither smart nor brave. I've been working out a way to do it."

"Dear God!" Devon ran to him and threw her arms around him.

Brother and sister held each other for several minutes, Devon sobbing.

"Crunch time has arrived, folks," Brent finally announced.

They both stared at him.

"Here's what we have to do."

Twenty-Seven

Lawyers, whether they were called attorneys or solicitors, didn't appreciate being roused at six o'clock in the morning, but as Brent had learned, titles carried some weight. Mr. Josiah Harrington agreed to come to Viscount Kentler's flat within the hour.

Devon, in the only domestic chores Brent had ever seen her perform, prepared coffee and toast and set out a small buffet in Nolan's generally unused dining room. Mr Harrington was a middle-aged man of average height with a fringe of graying hair, a smooth face and intelligent brown eyes.

He listened patiently to the narratives Brent, Nolan and Devon recounted, asked a series of penetrating questions, then put in a call to Sir William Bradshaw, the Hunter family's barrister. By ten o'clock formal statements had been given and signed by the three at New Scotland Yard and a search warrant had been issued covering all the properties owned or under the purview of Charles Robinett, the Duke of Camberg. The judge also signed an order of arrest and detention for the nobleman.

"There have been other accusations leveled against His Grace," Mr. Harrington told Brent as they were leaving police headquarters, "but they have always been quashed before advancing this far. Still, this matter is far from over. Camberg will retain powerful counsel and will undoubtedly contest with infuriating meticulousness every element of every charge made against him. It has been my experience, however, that in cases of this nature, the fight itself often produces unexpected results, leading authorities to matters they had heretofore not considered."

"And what of my brother?" Devon asked. Nolan had already left with Sir William.

"He won't get off, if that's what you're hoping," Harrington responded sympathetically. "Nonetheless I believe I can show that many, if not most, of his illicit actions, while technically performed of his own free will, were in fact carried out under duress. That may serve to mitigate to some degree the depth of his culpability. He won't be charged with driving under the influence, since that can't be proved. The fundamental charge of hit-and-run, however, is still a very serious offense, especially in light of the death of the victim. We have only his word that the man died instantly and that nothing could be done to save him. Exhumation of the body, if there is one, may or may not confirm the claim."

"Will he be sent to prison?" Brent asked.

The solicitor nodded. "I think it a virtual certainty. With his cooperation, we may be able to minimize the term."

"Lady Kestler—"

"Sir William will personally apprise her of the situation. And you, sir. May I ask your plans? In the unlikely event we need more information or finer detail, where can we find you?"

Brent gave the name of his hotel. "But I'll probably be returning to the States in the next day or two. I'll call your office and leave word of my travel plans as soon as I finalize them."

"Thank you, Mr. Preston. I appreciate your cooperation. And you, Miss Hunter?" he asked Devon.

"I'm stopping at Pathwatch Hall, then I'll be returning to Oxford." They'd reached the street. A taxi approached and she put out her hand. "You can call my mother if you need to find me," she said as she opened the back door and fled inside.

Brent considered following her but doubted he'd be welcome in Lady Kestler's house, and the fact that Devon had left without saying a word to him was indication enough that she wasn't interested in his company.

"Can I drop you, Mr. Preston?" Harrington asked, as he waved down a second cab. "Your hotel is on my way."

To refuse without good reason would have been impolite. Besides, this gave Brent a chance to pose some questions he'd hesitated to raise in Devon's presence.

"How do you see this matter working out, Mr. Harrington?" he asked when they were under way.

"Lord Kestler says he will plead guilty, which I think in the circumstances is a wise decision. His cooperation will save the Crown considerable time and expense and no doubt earn him a lighter sentence. Sir William can be very persuasive, and since Lord Kestler has no previous record of misbehavior, I would expect a five-year term, most if not all of it on probation."

"And Charles Robinett?"

"I hesitate to guess. He has a long record of accusations against him, but no formal charges and no convictions, so the accusations will probably be disallowed at trial. The evidence against him is serious, but in my opinion it will all turn on whether the witnesses are willing to be upstanding in court. Miss Hunter will be formidable, if she's willing to face him."

"She will," Brent said confidently.

Once inside his hotel room, he placed a call to his father.

"So it's over," Thomas said.

Between Devon and me, too, Brent thought, but this wasn't about him. It was about the honor of the family.

"Your mother wants to speak to you," his father said a moment later.

Brent could hear the phone being passed.

"What about Devon?" Jenna asked. "How is she?"

"She's with her mother now. It's not a very happy time for either of them."

"How do you feel about her?"

It wasn't an easy question to answer. He'd offered his help and twice she'd rejected it. Her cooperation at the end was only because she saw no alternative. And yet…she'd been willing to sacrifice everything, even what she felt for him, to save the honor of *her* family, people who in his estimation weren't worthy of her. But that wasn't the point. What was he willing to give up for his family, for his daughters? Everything. Maybe the answer to his mother's question wasn't so difficult after all.

"I love her, Mom."

"Then go after her." When Brent said nothing, Jenna asked quietly, "How do you think she feels about you?"

Brent nearly sighed. "She's past the angry stage, maybe even past the hurt stage. She just wants me out of her life."

"She may think so now, but—"

"I'll call you back as soon as I have my arrival time tomorrow. Give the girls a big hug for me."

"I'm glad you're here," Sir William told Devon. They were in the foyer of Pathwatch Hall. Perkins, the butler, was helping him into his overcoat. "Your mother will require a great deal of support from you over the next difficult months."

Devon thanked the barrister for his help and went into the library where her mother spent most of her time. Beyond the leaded casement windows lay the garden. In the spring it would blaze with color that would last most of the summer and into the autumn. Now, however, it was draped in winter gray.

Sarah Hunter sat in her motorized chair staring out over the drab landscape.

"How are you, Mother?"

The elderly woman turned her head. "Not one of my better days. Come sit down."

Devon settled onto the cushion-covered bench of the bay alcove. She should say something consoling but had no idea what.

"I understand Charles threatened you," her mother said.

Devon nodded.

"I wish you had said something to me. I would have got you protection. We could have fought him earlier. Maybe then some of this might not have happened."

So her mother was placing the blame on her. The unfairness of it should make her angry, but she was beyond feeling anything.

"I went to Nolan, Mother, expecting him to protect me, but he didn't, though he knew what kind of man I was forced to deal with. Or are you blaming me, too, for Nolan's drunk driving, for his defrauding people out of their money, for his willingness to conspire with a member of the aristocracy?"

"You're angry with me," Sarah said, "and you have every right to be. I haven't been a very good mother. If I had, Nolan wouldn't be facing prison, and you wouldn't be miserable."

Why was it her mother made it sound as if it was all about poor Sarah, even when she was offering a mea culpa?

"I'm not miserable," Devon argued. "I'm just glad this travesty is over. At least for me. What happens to Nolan now is of his own doing."

"Do you hate *him,* too?"

"No, Mother, I don't hate anybody. I'm beyond hate. I've reached the point of indifference."

Her mother didn't challenge the statement.

Silence lingered between the two women for several minutes. Devon was about to get up and leave when her mother asked, "What about your young man?"

"My young man?"

"Mr. Preston. It was quite obvious when you brought him here that he has feelings for you." Then she added with a wan smile, "And that you have feelings for him."

Devon wasn't sure if she was surprised or annoyed at her mother's perceptiveness. Not that it made any difference. "He's going home to his family."

"And you'll allow him to leave you?"

"Why shouldn't I?"

"Because if you do, you'll regret it for the rest of your life."

When Devon failed to respond, Lady Kestler went on. "Why do you think you're not worthy of him?"

"I don't know what you're talking about, Mother."

"Oh, I think you do. You think because your brother is about to be sent to prison, because he stole from the Prestons and dishonored himself, he also dishonored you and has made you unworthy."

"There's more to it than that," Devon snapped. At her mother's inquiring glance, she said, "When Charles threatened me, I caved in. Just like Nolan. I let him intimidate me instead of standing up to him."

"You were scared, and you were weak."

"More than weak, I was cowardly." Devon laughed. "Like Nolan, I retreated when I should have charged headlong and fought."

"Aggressive defense doesn't seem to be a family trait, does it?" Lady Kestler agreed with a humorless laugh. "But you have the power to change that, darling. I certainly haven't been a good example, and as you point out, Nolan hasn't been, either. But this man, Preston, he seems to me to be a fine model of perseverance and spunk. I understand he broke the nose of one of his attackers at Morningfield Manor."

"You know about that?"

Sarah smiled with amusement this time and nodded. "He's a man who can inspire, and I suspect one who won't allow you to wallow in misgivings."

"I'm not wallowing," Devon objected, but of course

that was exactly what she was doing. "I have nothing to offer him."

"Are you sure?"

Again there was a long pause filled with silence.

"For one thing, you have beauty, which I never had. It still amazes me that this ugly duckling could have given birth to such a lovely swan. And because I was what was politely called plain, I sold myself short."

Devon gazed at her mother with fresh eyes. It was true she wasn't a physically attractive woman, but Devon had never given it much consideration. It seemed to her Sarah Morningfield had made up for it with dignity—if not charm—and sophistication.

"What I had in my youth was money, piles of it, thanks to my father, who seemed to have a Midas knack for accumulating it even during the hardest of times. I saw myself as a rich troll, so that when the poor man I cared for offered me his hand in marriage, I was convinced it was for the wealth I could bring, and I turned him away. Later, when Nigel asked me to marry him, I was convinced it had to be for love. He was a viscount, after all. Trouble is, I had it backward. Philip was the one who'd loved me for who I was. It was Nigel who was after my money."

Devon was stunned and fascinated. Her mother had never told her about this before. That there might have been someone in her life before her father had never occurred to her.

"The one thing I did right," Sarah said, "was to keep control of my father's inheritance. You probably think I've hoarded it, and maybe I have. I know Nolan feels that way. Maybe one day he'll realize his shortcomings have never been financial but moral, like his father's."

The old woman adjusted the folds of her dress, uncharacteristically avoiding eye contact with her daughter.

"I never had the physical or emotional strength to fight your father," she continued, "and so I hid behind my weakness. I seem to have bequeathed that cowardice to Nolan, as well. But it doesn't have to be your legacy."

"I don't understand," Devon said.

"You blame yourself for not standing up to Camberg, and I have to admit you should have, but you made up for it when Preston attacked your brother's reputation. You stood by Nolan even though he had failed you. Even when it became clear he was in serious trouble, you didn't back down from pursuing the truth. That took strength, my dear, courage and a sense of values."

Devon appreciated what her mother was saying, but she still didn't buy it.

"Hardly," she said with a scoff. "When Charles showed up with more threats, I again backed away."

"To protect me," her mother reminded her. "Before you arrived, Sir William told me about Charles's ridiculous charge that I was part of your brother's fraudulent enterprise."

"I never believed it," Devon protested.

"I should hope not. The point is, you were willing to give up the man you loved because you felt an obligation to protect me even though I have failed you all these years."

Devon rose and paced the area between the two bay windows. The man she loved. Yes, it was true, but…

"Has *he* pushed you away?" the older woman asked. "Preston, I mean. Has he rejected you, suggested he isn't interested in being with you?"

"No, but—"

"You don't feel worthy of him," Sarah stated. "Is that it?"

"I'm hardly someone he can be proud of."

"Why don't you let him decide that?"

Twenty-Eight

Brent called home. It was late afternoon in England, mid-morning in Kentucky. His mother answered the phone.

"I'll be getting into Louisville at eight tomorrow morning your time."

"What about Devon?"

"What about her?" he asked.

"Have you seen her?"

"She doesn't want to see me, Mother."

"How do you know that?"

"Because she walked away without even saying good-bye, that's why."

"Men," Jenna expostulated. "Did it ever occur to you that she didn't say goodbye because she wants you to come after her?"

Brent held the phone away from his ear and stared at

it. "No, it didn't," he finally said, putting it back in place, "because that would be—"

"Go after her, Brent. That poor girl is suffering, and you've left her to do it alone. I don't know what it is about men that makes them so insensitive. It's as plain as the nose on your face—"

"You're serious, aren't you?"

"Of course I'm serious. For heaven's sake, Brent. She feels she's unworthy of you. Her family is in disgrace. She thinks you're ashamed of her."

"Ashamed? That's ridiculous!"

"Have you told her that?" When he didn't reply, she said, "Go after her, son. Let her know she's worth pursuing."

He huffed. "I'm not sure where she is."

"And a big, smart man like you can't find out?" she asked sarcastically.

"Now I'm smart. A minute ago you said I was stupid."

Jenna sighed. "I said you were insensitive. Now, where is she likely to be?"

"She was going over to her mother's house—"

"That sounds like a good place to start, son."

"It's a Mr. Preston on the line, milady," Perkins said.

"Oh, well, let me speak to him."

The butler brought her the cordless phone.

"Mr. Preston…"

"I'm sorry to disturb you, Lady Kestler, but I'm looking for your daughter."

"She's not here, I'm afraid. She spoke with Mr. Harrington, and he said you were leaving on the six o'clock flight from Heathrow. She's on her way there."

"To see me?"

"She doesn't know anyone else flying out of the country this evening that I'm aware of."

"Actually, I'm not leaving, either. I called a few minutes ago and changed my booking to tomorrow. I was hoping to see her."

"You'll find her at the airport. I suggest you hurry, Mr. Preston, or you'll be passing each other in opposite directions."

Devon scanned the crowd at the international ticket counters, but she didn't see him. He must have already gone through security to his gate. A uniformed agent was tapping quietly on a computer keyboard at the first-class section.

"Can you tell me if Brent Preston has checked in yet? He's an American, going to—"

He continued to tap on the keyboard. "No, miss, I cannot. I'm not allowed to give out the status of passengers."

"But how can I find out if he's here?"

"Not my problem."

She glared at him, but he either didn't notice or didn't care.

"That's a very unprofessional attitude," she said sharply.

"And you're going to find yourself in custody for making a disturbance in a public place, if you don't step away." This time he did meet her eyes, and she had no doubt he meant it.

"How—"

"Step back, miss, or I'll call security."

Genuinely frightened by his threat, she did as she was told. Dammit, she thought, here I am giving up again. She was about to challenge the officious clerk, devil take the hindmost, when a woman in the line beside her said, "Try paging him, dear."

She stared at the short, dumpy woman for a moment before the words sank in. "Oh, yes, of course. Page him. Yes, I will. Thank you," she said gratefully.

"The phones are right over there." The woman pointed to a bank of instruments at the far end of the long terminal. "Good luck, dearie."

The cab had barely come to a stop when Brent jumped out, having already given the driver the fare plus the generous tip he'd promised for getting him to the terminal in record time. The flight he had been booked on was due to depart in a matter of minutes. Once it took off, Devon would leave, figuring he was on it. Then it would be off to Oxford to track her down there. But he'd rather spend the time with her here instead of on a train. He'd tried calling her on her cell phone, but she either had it turned off or had it on vibrate in her coat pocket and couldn't feel it ring.

He barged through the automatic doors into the international terminal, and almost knocked down an old man struggling with two suitcases on wheels.

"Mind where you're going," the man grumbled angrily.

"Sorry," Brent called back as he continued making his way toward the counter, scanning the crowd for Devon.

He approached an agent fiddling with a computer keyboard. "Have you seen—"

The man ignored him.

"You're the American," a dumpling of a woman in the neighboring line said and smiled at him. She pointed down the line. "She went that way to the phones."

The man at her side said, "Go get her, mate."

Brent sprinted in the direction she indicated, dodging around people, apologizing, bumping into others in his mad haste to find her.

Then he saw her, or rather the back of her head, as she lifted a courtesy phone. He stopped behind her, barely resisting the urge to touch.

"Looking for someone?"

"Yes, I—" she said anxiously, spinning around.

She stood there, still as a statue, with the phone in her hand. "Brent…"

He gazed at her, convinced now he couldn't let her go. She was a part of him. "Devon…"

"Are you using that phone, miss?"

She started and glanced blankly at the stranger standing next to Brent. "Oh, no, not now. Sorry." Without looking, she handed the man the receiver and took a step to the side.

Brent tucked his fingers under her arm and coaxed her away.

"I was afraid I'd missed you," she murmured, still staring up at him.

"I'm not going anywhere…without you."

"But your flight—"

"Tomorrow or the next day or the day after that or however long it takes for me to convince you to come with me."

"Go with you? Where?"

"Home, Devon. To Kentucky. To the girls. To the most beautiful place in the world. I want you there, at my side, as my wife, as the mother of my children."

She stared at him, as if she were in a trance.

"I meant what I said, Devon. I love you. And now I'm asking you to marry me."

"But…"

"Unless you don't love me. You haven't said—"

"Oh, I do, Brent. I do love you."

He took her in his arms then and kissed her. Hard.

There was applause and good-natured laughter around them. They broke off, red-faced.

"We seem to be drawing a crowd," he said.

"I wonder why."

"Let's go back to my hotel. We can talk there…in private, and…well, do other things."

She laughed then, and the happy sound that had captured him from the start curled its way deeper inside him, making him almost light-headed.

He escorted her through the terminal entrance. Getting a cab took only a minute. He kissed her as they returned to the city and babbled on about the great future they had before them, how much she would love Kentucky, how happy his folks would be to see her get off the plane with him, and how ecstatic the girls would be to have a new mom.

When they arrived at the hotel, however, she hung back when he tried to squire her to the elevator.

"I'm not sure this is wise," she said, not meeting his eyes.

He stopped dead in his tracks and regarded her, so serious and so obviously troubled. "Surely you're not concerned about Camberg. He's—"

She shook her head. "No, he has no power over me anymore. He never should have. But—"

"But what?"

"This is all happening so fast, Brent. How well do we really know each other?"

He was tempted to say, *Let's go upstairs and find out,*

but the expression on her face discouraged levity. "I know I love you. You said you love me. Isn't that enough?"

"Do you?" she asked.

He stared at her and for a moment wondered if she might be right, that they didn't know each other at all. If they did, how could she ask this question?

"Let's sit down," he suggested, matching her somber tone.

He waved to a secluded corner of the lobby, dread twisting inside him when only a few seconds before he'd felt exhilaration.

"Tell me what's bothering you," he said, when they were seated on chairs separated by an end table, their knees almost knocking. He took her hand. "Please."

She pulled it away, and suddenly it all came spilling out. His lying to her initially about why he had come to England and the reason for his presence at Briar Hills Academy. Not telling her how he had found out about Texas Tea. But it wasn't all an indictment against him. She questioned how he could possibly burden himself—and his children—with a woman whose brother was a felon, with a woman who had cowered under the vile threats of a bully instead of standing up to him and fighting. How could he possibly love a coward?

As he listened to her, he wished more than ever that they were in his room, so he could gather her in his arms and hold her tight. He ached to soothe away the worry marring her beautiful face, kiss away the tears that hung poised in her brown eyes.

"I'm not perfect, Devon," he finally said. "You may have noticed that. It's true I deceived you when I first got here, but my deception wasn't aimed at you."

"It was, Brent," she retorted. "The only reason you came to Briar Hills Academy was to see me, to spy on me, to use me to destroy my brother."

He hung his head. She was right from her perspective.

"That was because I didn't know you," he said, hoping he could make her understand. "You were a name, not a person. I didn't know if you were going to be an ally or an enemy. I certainly didn't know I was going to fall in love with you. But once I did—"

"What about the trip to Dorset?" she interrupted. "By then you knew me, enough at least to make love to me."

"That was a mistake. Not the making love part," he hastened to clarify. "How could I possibly regret making love to you? I want to spend the rest of my life making love to you, Devon. But the trip to Dorset… I should have told you up front what I knew and how I knew it."

"Why didn't you?"

How could he possibly tell her that even though he loved her then, he still wasn't sure he could trust her?

"Because I didn't trust my own judgment," he acknowledged. "If I had it to do over again, I would tell you. Everything. Once we got there, though, I didn't hold anything back, because by then I knew, that no matter how much it hurt, you were committed to doing the right thing. And you did. As for your brother…"

He paused. "Like you, I imagine, I have mixed feelings. He did a lot of stupid, dishonest things that nearly destroyed my family, things that endangered your life and your happiness, yet many of them he did to protect you, too. I suspect when it's all over you'll forgive him, if you haven't already. And if you can be that generous, I'll try to be, as well."

"It's all so unfair," she mumbled.

Brent watched a tear fall and couldn't stand it anymore. He couldn't bear to see her so miserable. He climbed to his feet, stood over her and extended his hands. Shyly, she placed hers in them, and he pulled her up so that she was standing mere inches from him.

"Let me tell you what I think about your last charge," he said, his lips so close he didn't have to speak above a whisper. "You're not a coward, Devon. You're one of the bravest women I've ever met. You've endured coldness, yet remained warm. You've been abused and rejected, yet you're willing to sacrifice to protect, and you're willing to forgive. I want to spend the rest of my life being worthy of your strength and courage, your goodness and love."

She pressed her cheek against his chest. "Oh, Brent…"

"Now, will you please come up to my room with me? We have telephone calls to make."

"Is that all?" She looked up, smiling through her tears.

He grinned. "What do you think?" He kissed the tip of her nose. "I love you, Devon. I'll love you for the rest of my life."

Epilogue

"We're doing very well," Thomas said, now that everyone had the drinks of their choice, and the children had gone to bed. He swirled his Scotch on the rocks. "I never expected us to recover quite as fast as we have. Our occupancy is already up to ninety percent of last year's peak."

"Training's at eight-five percent," Robbie announced. He was drinking port.

"Breeding contracts are only at about seventy-five percent," Brent admitted, pleased to be drinking Bourbon again. "And revenue is less than fifty percent of last year, but that's because of the discounts I've offered. Next year will be considerably better. I expect we'll come close to matching last season, if not exceed it."

"Even with overall revenues down, we're already in the black for this year," Thomas said, "and that isn't counting the check from Lady Kestler."

"That certainly was a surprise," Jenna remarked.

Brent laughed. "I don't think I've ever seen that many zeros in a row on one check."

"Your mother was very generous," Jenna told Devon.

Devon took a sip of her sherry. "She said it was only fair, since that was what you estimated your cash losses to be from Nolan's fraud."

"How is he doing?"

"Quite well, actually. Since Mother agreed to pay all the damages, he was sentenced to only five years. The solicitor says he'll have to serve about two of them in prison, maybe less. The rest will be on probation."

"I suppose it's a small price to pay," Marcus said, "considering the millions it cost other people and must be costing his mother now. I used to resent him, and maybe a part of me always will, but a part of me feels sorry for him, too. All that wealth and privilege, yet I had something he never had. A mother's love."

He and his half sister, Devon, had finally met today. He looked at her now and smiled. "And a sister's love he never appreciated. Poor man."

"What about Camberg?" Andrew asked. "Surely he didn't get away scott-free?"

"His house of cards collapsed when Nolan opened up," Brent explained. "One bit of information led to another and the evidence against him piled up like snow drifts in a blizzard. My noticing the tattoo on the wrist of my assailant in the garden at Morningfield Manor, for instance, tied in with the attack against Melanie, as well as the shenanigans with Lord Rochester's horse in Dubai. The tattoo marks members of an international mafia. Several of its members have sworn statements incriminating Camberg, and Interpol has been able to seize records at his retreat in southern France. He's going to be a guest of Her Majesty for many, many years."

"Too bad it's come at such a terrible cost to others," Jenna remarked quietly.

"I understand your brother's losing Morningfield Manor, as well," Melanie remarked to Devon.

Devon nodded. "When Mother found out he planned to sell the estate on her death, she decided to give it to me instead."

"A nice wedding present," Melanie noted.

"Except she insists I take possession of it before we get married—"

"That way you can keep it if the marriage doesn't work out," Brent explained. "Very wise."

"Still manipulating, eh?" Thomas snorted.

Devon laughed. "Old habits are hard to break."

"Just protecting her daughter," Brent countered. "Better late than never. Good for her, I say."

"She suggested we get married there, as well," Devon commented, "but I said no. This is my new home. She did agree to come to the wedding, though, so prepare yourselves!"

Everyone laughed.

"Tell me, Dad," Thomas said to his father as he poured him a bit more Jameson, "did you ever expect anyone in our family to have an estate, complete with stables and a castle, in England?"

Hugh's faded blue eyes twinkled. "If I'd wanted to be in England, son, I'd have crossed the Irish Sea instead of the Atlantic Ocean. I have no regrets. None at all."

Thoroughbred Legacy

The purse is set and the stakes are high,…
Romance, scandal and glamour set in the
exhilarating world of horse-racing!

The Legacy continues with book #8

A LADY'S LUCK

by Ken Casper

In England to investigate the breeding scandal surrounding his
stables, head breeder Brent Preston finds himself intrigued by
Devon Hunter—the sister of a man he suspects is involved. As
they unravel the mystery together, they are unable to deny their
attraction…until imminent danger threatens their newfound love.

*Look for A LADY'S LUCK
in September 2008 wherever books are sold.*